The Town

Of Patches

a novel by

WALTER FRIEND

ISBN: 9781724187949

This book is dedicated to the memory of my father. Wish you were here. Special thanks to my family for believing in me. I love you all.

CONTENTS

Chapter I
The Perfect Pumpkin

"Dad, can we go pick out the pumpkin now?"

"That's where we're going, Johnny. We had breakfast at Tuby's. The blueberry waffles were yummy. What the...." Dad swerved the car, and we skidded off the road into the side of a wheat field.

I dropped my half-eaten candy bar, and gooey chocolate ran down my skull tee shirt. The tall grass bounced against the station wagon, and we came to an abrupt stop. Smoke fumed off the tires. "What's wrong?"

Dad grabbed my wrist and said sharply, "Did you see the woman lying down in the middle of the road? I would have hit her if I didn't turn off."

"No, I didn't see her. I wasn't paying attention until you crashed." I turned around to look out the back window. "I can't see anything except the wheat field."

"Hold on!" Dad backed the car up and parked along the side of the road. "She's over there." He pointed at her while unbuckling his seat belt. "I think she needs help. Johnny, I want you to stay here!"

"No, I want to help."

Dad shook his head. "Not this time, son. I will be back in a minute."

As I watched Dad walk toward the woman, I started thinking about my good-deed merit badge that I was trying to get for Boy

Scouts. If I help that woman, the badge is mine. I slammed the car door shut and walked over to Dad. He was standing above the woman.

"Should we help her up?" I asked.

Dad looked mad. "Johnny, what are you doing? I told you to stay in the car!"

"You know how I've been trying to get my good-deed merit badge. This is the best deed I could think of."

Dad smirked. "You are crazy, boy! I can't believe I'm doing this. You can stay."

She was wearing a purple nightgown splattered with mud. Her long, snow-white hair resembled a lion's mane, stopping just above her bottom.

Dad poked her. "Hey, lady, are you okay?"

She slowly turned over, and her face looked like a living skeleton. The sight of her was very disturbing. She wiped some dirt off her bony nose and reddened cheeks. The way she stared at us with her cold, black eyes sent a chill down my back. She ran her fingers through her fine, white hair and flipped it. She gave us a relieved smile, raised her head, and whispered, "Now, I am. My boys are coming home." Her eyes rolled back, and she collapsed with a thud into the pavement.

Dad grabbed her shoulders and tried to shake her awake.

She didn't respond.

"Wake up!" he shouted over and over, until tears appeared in the corners of his eyes. He began to administer CPR. He shook his head sadly. "She didn't make it. We have to call the sheriff. I saw a gas station with a pay phone, a few miles back."

I shrugged off another chill. I never realized my Dad was such an emotional man. He cried for her, and he didn't even know her. I just stood there like a fool.

"We should cover her, out of respect and get her out of the road. I think there is a blanket in the car," Dad said. We walked back to the car. Dad popped the trunk open to get the blanket. We returned to the woman, covered her, and carried her body to the side of the road. As we drove to the gas station, I hammered Dad with questions about the woman. "What do you think she meant when she said, 'My boys are coming home'"?

"Maybe she was talking about her kids."

"I got that feeling too. Do you think she was hit by a car?"

"No. I didn't see any bruises. It looked like she crawled out of a hole in the ground. She had so much mud on her," Dad explained.

"I guess you're right." I could see beads of sweat breaking on Dad's brow even though it was cool in the car.

"Johnny, I need you to be quiet right now!"

I frowned. "Okay."

Dad made the call. We didn't say a word to each other on the way back from the gas station. At least he bought me a pop. When we arrived back at the body, we just stood around staring at her with our hands in our pockets. I couldn't believe no one found her while we were gone.

Dad finally broke the silence when he saw a slow-driving police car in the distance. "I'm sorry you had to see this, son."

My emotions finally caught up with me. "How horrible. She's dead!" I exclaimed with a lump in my throat.

Dad hugged me and messed up my hair. "She was a nice lady. She went to heaven."

The sheriff parked his cruiser. As he strutted toward us, I noticed how tough he looked with his lumberjack build, beaming eyes, and dangling gun. He looked happy to see us. He couldn't stop smiling. I found his demeanor strange. How could he not know that a woman died? Didn't Dad tell him?

"Roden, is that you?" asked the sheriff.

"Yeah, it's me, Kennedy Shiberblat. It's been a long time."

Dad reached out his hand for the sheriff to shake.

Kennedy shook his head. "You're not getting off that easy. We were best friends growing up." He grabbed Dad and gave him a big hug.

Dad patted him on the back then pulled away. "I missed you. How many years has it been?"

"It's got to be twenty," Dad answered. "Last I heard you were in Vermont. I wasn't sure if I was ever going to run into you again. I just wish the timing was better. You look good."

"Thanks Roden, you too."

"Kennedy, we have to take care of this then we'll catch up." Dad looked down at the blanket-covered body. My boy and I found her dying in the road. After she died, we covered her."

Kennedy's eyes widened.

"Before I look, who's this guy?"

"That's Johnny. He's my son."

"Give me five, Slim."

I slapped his hand.

"How old are you?"

"Twelve," my voice cracked.

"Wow, Roden! I can't believe you have a son this old."

"A lot of time has gone by, old friend." Dad stared off into a passing cloud.

"You're right. Two decades is a long time. I see you are wearing a wedding band. Do I know your wife?"

"I don't think so. She's not from around here. You should come over some time and meet her."

"I'm there, buddy. Do you have more kids?"

"No, just Johnny. He's the best son a guy could have."

I looked at Dad warmly. It was incredible what he had said.

"What about you? A wife, kids?" Dad asked.

"A nomad never settles down."

"What's a nomad?" I asked.

"A wanderer," Kennedy answered.

"When did you become the sheriff of Whisper?" Dad asked.

"I came back to Connecticut three years ago. I've been the sheriff for two. Want to see me spin my gun?"

Dad made a stop sign with his hand. "No, that's okay. We don't want to give Johnny any bad ideas. It amazes me Kennedy, that it took this long for us to run into each other."

"I know what you mean. Whisper is such a small town."

"What else? Tell me more."

"There's not a lot to tell. I was living in Vermont for a long time climbing mountains and chasing dreams. The last time we saw each other we were your boy's age. What happened to us? Why didn't we keep in touch?"

I had to say something. Nobody was discussing why we were here. "Um … guys … I hate to break up your reunion." I pointed to the blanket-covered woman. "What about her?"

The sheriff winked at me. "You're right, John, back to work." He took a peek. "Oh my God! You guys! You found her."

I snuck another look. Her body had turned death's pasty color.

Dad saw what I was doing. He yanked my hooded sweatshirt, pulling me back. "Stop it! You'll get nightmares." He gave Kennedy a confused look. "Found who?"

"Lucille Bipimtaff." He shook his head. "Not a nice lady. She disappeared a few months ago. Did she say anything?"

"One thing. It was strange. Her exact words were 'My boys are coming home' then she died," Dad answered.

Kennedy jotted this down in his notepad and took a second look at the woman. "It's her all right." He covered her back up with the blanket.

"Excuse me, Sheriff, what do you think she was trying to say?" I asked.

"Your boy is well-mannered, Roden." Kennedy winked at me. "Ask your father. He knows her."

Dad rolled his eyes at Kennedy. "What! What are you saying? I don't. I don't know her!"

Kennedy swatted a mosquito away from his shirt. "You got to watch those autumn skitters. They can make you sick. You really don't remember her. Do you?"

"No."

"Here's a hint: 1940 Halloween carnival."

I turned to my father. "How come you have never taken me to a Halloween carnival?"

"Johnny, Whisper stopped doing Halloween carnivals when Kennedy and I were children."

I frowned. "That stinks. I want to go to one. It would have been a blast with Halloween coming up next week."

Kennedy gave Dad an intense look. "Roden, why did Whisper stop the Halloween carnivals?"

Dad looked like he was getting mad. "I told you before! I don't remember!"

"When someone dies in front of you, it makes you forget. I know, it's happened to me. I don't think you got a good enough look at her. I want you to look again."

"Kennedy, what are you trying to start?" Dad flipped the blanket off the dead woman for another look. He studied her up and down for a good minute before slumping down into the road. "How did this happen? Why didn't I recognize her before?"

Kennedy picked Dad up off the road. He kept his arm around him. "Tell me who she is." One of Kennedy's buttons popped off the top of his tight uniform shirt. The metal button clinked on the pavement and rolled on its side before coming to a stop. We all just stood and watched it. "Spit it out, Roden!"

Dad hesitated but finally answered. "She's the mother of the three boys that were tragically killed at the Halloween carnival. The ones who fell to their deaths from the top of the cliff."

"I bet you feel better now that you've gotten that off your chest."

"Why do you have to bring up old wounds?" Dad wouldn't even look Kennedy in the eye. He just stared at the ground. "And just so you know, I don't feel better."

Kennedy let go of Dad to make a swinging motion with an invisible bat. "Roden, you hit the ball out of the park." When Lucille's sons died, Halloween carnivals ended in Whisper."

"That's sad. Who got killed?" I asked.

Dad snapped at me. "Johnny! Give the questions a rest, okay?"

I made a pig-nose face at Dad. I thought he would laugh, but he gave me a stone face back.

Dad poked Kennedy in the chest. "I don't want to hear about what happened at the carnival when we were kids. It was tragic that those boys died. Leave it at that!"

Why was Dad acting so weird about Lucille and her boys while Kennedy was so open about everything? What happened at that Halloween carnival? Something is not right.

In a calmer voice, Dad asked. "So why was Lucille missing?"

"I only had a few run-ins with her besides that one time when we were kids. You guys want to hear about what she did a few months ago?"

"It was nice seeing you again, Kennedy, but this is too much." Dad tapped me on the shoulder. "Johnny, let's go."

"I don't want to. I want to hear about her. I'm not afraid."

"*Bang bang*," said Kennedy, making a gun with his finger. He pointed it at me. "Good for you, Slim. I knew you were a tough guy."

Dad gave Kennedy a look that could have frozen the world. "You're supposed to be the sheriff!" he spat. "What kind of lawman are you anyway?"

"I like to live on the edge. You know ... like when we were kids. We use to do some crazy things."

Dad looked stressed out. "We're not kids." He pushed both his hands through his salt and pepper hair. His forehead creased. "Let me think."

"Please, Dad," I begged with a conning grin. "I want to hear the story."

"Ten, twenty, or fifty years can go by. I remember us being kids like yesterday. Please, Dad," Kennedy implored with the same grin.

"Man, you are so messed up." Dad's mood flip-flopped, and he winked at Kennedy. I guess he wanted to hear the story after all. "Your story better not be too scary," he warned.

Kennedy got really close to Dad. "Boo! It's ghost-story scary."

I laughed. "Ghost stories. I love ghost stories.

Chapter 2
Lucille's Story

Kennedy chuckled. His eyes lit up like Fourth of July sparklers. He really wanted to tell us about Lucille Bipimtaff.

"It all started about six months ago. I was driving one night down Kings Highway."

I interrupted. "Hey, guys, we're on that road." I pointed. "The sign is over there above that bush."

"Johnny, would you let the man tell his story?"

"Oh, sorry."

"It was pouring rain and a little after midnight when I pulled up to a woman who was walking along the side of the street in nothing but a nightgown. I thought maybe she was sleepwalking. As if that wasn't strange enough, she was also carrying a brightly lit candle. What kind of candle burns in the rain?"

"A magic candle," I answered.

"A trick candle," Dad answered.

"Good answers, but I really don't know what kind of candle burns in the rain. I rolled down the window and waved her over. Water splashed into the car. She held the glowing candle a few inches from my face. I watched the raindrops bounce off the flame. I pinched myself over and over again to make sure I wasn't dreaming. Her long, white hair was dripping wet and glued around her wrinkled face.

At first she looked like a sweet lady, maybe in her late fifties, but after I got a good look at her, I changed my mind. She was very scary with cracked red eyes. Maybe she hadn't slept in days, been drinking, or was on drugs."

"Need some help?" I asked. "She tilted her head while gripping the car window with both hands. She entered some kind of trance because I watched her red eyes turn black, and her face turned pale as a ghost. I unholstered my gun. She was getting a little too close for comfort. A lot of rain was coming into the car. She asked me in a panicked voice, 'Have you seen my boys?' I answered: 'No, I haven't seen anyone. How could you in this heavy rain?'

I wish I never said that. She dropped the candle then attacked me through the window like a villain on a rampage. I raised my gun. She knocked it out of my hand. Her wet hair felt like worms sliming on my body, and her swinging hands felt like cold steel gloves. I wondered how this woman could have the strength of a titan!"

She screamed, 'My boys! My boys! Have you seen them?' I wrestled with her trying to break free until she punched me in the head. I blacked out. There's no feeling in the world like being knocked out by a possessed old lady. I woke up in the car wrestling myself."

"Wow! That's a crazy story, Sheriff," I said, biting my lip.

The sheriff flipped up his hair to show us the goose egg she left him.

"How disturbing. And to think ... I thought she was a nice lady. I tried to save her," Dad said.

"I hate to say this, but I'm glad she's dead."

Dad made a stop sign with his hand. "Don't say that, Kennedy. That's bad karma."

"Whatever, Roden. She could have killed me. I still don't know why she didn't. I really thought about what she was saying: 'Have you seen my boys?' Those words wouldn't stop repeating in my ears. Then it hit me. She was the mother of the Bipimtaff brothers. I know you don't want to hear this, but I remember at the Halloween carnival when Lucille lost her mind after the sheriff told her that her sons were dead. I know you remember too."

"I can still see her on the ground swearing at the crowd and crying, and all the people watching her like she was a tragic movie star. Her words: 'My boys, my boys, why did you kill my boys?' She kept blaming the crowd for their deaths. Nobody said anything. Nobody knew anything about how her sons fell off the top of the mountain."

"That's how I knew my attacker was Lucille. It was the way she talked about her boys. I went to her house with the deputy to arrest her for assaulting me. Nobody was home. Lucille must have abandoned her house months earlier by the three-foot-high grass growing in the yard. Come over to my squad car. I want to show you guys something."

We followed Kennedy to his car. Through the window we watched him throw newspapers and magazines across the front seat. He came back wielding a large knife. He handed it to Dad.

Dad ran his hand along the double-edged blade. "It's dull."

"It's supposed to be," Kennedy said.

"Why is the handle so heavy? It probably weighs five pounds. Why is it wrapped in black cloth?"

"The handle is used to absorb power. The more power obtained, the heavier the handle. This knife is called an athame. It's a witch's magical dagger. When a new witch is initiated into a coven, the members of the coven give the knife as a sacred gift."

"What's a coven?" I asked.

"House of witches," Kennedy answered.

"Why are you telling us this?" Dad wanted to know.

"You're still my best friend. You knew her, and she died in front of you. You deserve to know what's happening."

"Sheriff, are you saying Lucille is a witch?"

Kennedy pointed to the blanket-covered dead woman. "Yes, Slim. She was a powerful witch."

Dad lunged the knife toward Kennedy. As he was about to hit, he turned the blade downward, striking the sheriff lightly with his fist.

Kennedy ripped the blade from Dad's hand. "Give me that! I know we used to play that knife game when we were kids, but I'm the sheriff now. You have to let me know when you're going to do something insane like that."

Dad's grin turned upside down. "Are you done? Can we go now?"

"No, I didn't finish the story."

"Well, finish the freakin' story!"

I could smell the tension mounting. I wondered what kind of friends they were when they were kids. Seemed more like enemies to me.

Kennedy talked with his hands like he was directing a symphony. "So there we were, Deputy Strags and I. We had Lucille cornered with our guns pinned on her every move. Strags was standing next to the passenger door of the squad car. Lucille was in the middle and I was on the other side. She was dressed in the same purple nightgown as on the day she attacked me, and it was raining again. I let Strags take the lead."

"'All right, Mrs. Creep, hands up!' She couldn't understand anything he was saying. She just grunted over and over again. Strags looked confused. He turned to me, 'Sheriff, her eyes are black. She looks possessed.' I suggested we arrest her. Strags ordered her again: 'Lucille, put your hands up!' She ignored him."

"She stopped grunting and spoke in a croaky voice, 'Did you guys see three boys walking out here?' The deputy answered no before I could stop him. I don't know how she could have had this athame hidden under her nightgown. The blade on this thing has to be six inches." The sheriff waved the athame through the air. He pretended to stab Dad with it. *"Ha, ha. Got you back."*

Dad laughed. I guess they were friends.

"It happened so fast. She put the athame through the deputy's right hand. I heard the clunk as the blade stuck into the car door with Strags's hand attached to it. I fired my gun. So did my screaming deputy. Both guns misfired. How could that be? His pistol and mine broken at the same time. She disappeared again. I had the hardest time getting Strags unattached from the car door. We put her on our most wanted list."

"How tragic, Sheriff."

"Sure was, Slim."

"It gets stranger all the time," Dad grumbled. "Johnny, let's go."

"Wait. Don't you guys want to hear the rest?"

"Quickly," Dad answered.

"Do you know the big cemetery up the road from here?" Kennedy asked.

"Of course. Heaven's Cemetery. My Dad's buried there."

"Lucille's boys are buried there, too."

Dad took a handkerchief out of his jacket pocket. "I didn't know that." He blew his nose.

"I was sure we had her this time. Deputy Strags and myself caught Lucille climbing the cemetery wall with a shovel strapped to her back."

"That's unbelievable! Heaven's Cemetery walls are like sixteen feet high," Dad said.

I shook off a dark thought but asked it anyway. "Do you think she wanted to dig up her sons?"

"You have quite an imagination, Slim. She was scaling the wall like she had suction cups on her hands and feet. Strags begged to shoot her. 'No, I got her,' I responded. I jumped up and grabbed her by the foot. She wasn't wearing any shoes, and her feet smelled really bad."

"Yuck," I said.

"I figured she would fall then we could make our arrest," Kennedy smirked. "No chance," he shook his head.

"She continued climbing with me hanging from her leg. I ripped her nightgown. Pieces of cloth were flapping in the breeze. Where was she getting her strength from? Is she even human? I pleaded with her, 'Please come down! We won't hurt you.' She finally looked at me when she reached the top of the wall. Remember how her eyes were black and possessed?"

Dad and I were hypnotized by the sheriff's story. "Yeah," we said at the same time.

"Her eyes changed again. This time they had fiery flames coming out of them. It was as if she turned into some demon who had spawned up from hell. She spoke to us in a voice like finger nails down a chalk board. 'My boys are on the other side of this wall. I'm going to get them,' is what she said."

"The next thing I saw was a big foot kick me in the face. I fell and landed on my back in a pile of wet leaves. Strags started blasting. I heard ricocheting bullets and stones popping. I shined my flashlight across a wall. Lucille was gone. We searched every inch of the cemetery trying to find her. We even went to her sons' graves. I expected to see her digging in the midnight rain. This was not the case. Her sons' graves were untouched. I never found out where she was going with that shovel. That was the last time I saw Lucille until you guys found her. Now that she is dead, I guess she finally found her sons in Heaven or Hell."

"Probably Hell," Roden offered. "Kennedy, there is one thing I don't understand."

"What's that?"

"Why would you tell my son that story?"

"He saw her die. He deserves to know, just like you."

"He's twelve."

Kennedy let out a big smile. "I know."

"Sheriff, thanks for ..."

Dad stepped on my foot. "Don't say a word, Johnny! Kennedy, now I remember why I stopped hanging out with you. You are still crazy as hell!" Dad tightly frowned. "If you don't need us anymore, we are out of here."

The sheriff seemed disappointed.

"Roden, don't be like that. Lucille is dead. It's over," he explained.

I waived goodbye to the sheriff. On the way to the car, we ran into Deputy Strags. He didn't look tough like the sheriff. He had a nerdy appearance about him. It could have been from his big-as-a-planet nose and coke-bottle glasses. His right hand was wrapped in a bandage.

"Where you guys going?" asked the deputy.

Dad smirked. "We're out of here, Strags, but have a nice day!"

"Happy Halloween," I added.

"You too, young man," Strags replied.

The sheriff walked back over to us. "They can go," he told his deputy. "We don't need them. I have their statements. But I do need you to call the coroner immediately."

Dad got in his car and turned the key to the ignition. The engine coughed then hummed smoothly.

"When the sheriff said: 'Lucille is dead. It's over,' what did he mean?" I asked Dad.

He wasn't listening. He was eyeing my bottle of pop in the console. He gave it a shake. "You mind?"

I didn't say anything. By the look on his face as he drank, he was deep in thought. "Dad, are you going to answer me?"

"Forget what the sheriff just told you. It doesn't matter now. Leave it at that. Let's go get a pumpkin. "He stepped on the gas pedal, and the car lurched forward.

My head was spinning with everything that had happened. I tried to sort through my thoughts. Why did Dad not want me to know about Lucille, her sons, or the Halloween carnival? How do Dad and the sheriff know Lucille? What secrets are they hiding from the carnival? Did they know those boys who died? I know the sheriff said it was over, but I had a really bad feeling it wasn't. All of a sudden I felt sick. I cupped my hands against my stomach. "I don't feel so good," I told my father.

"Shake it off, tiger. We could forget about the pumpkin and go home."

"No way. I want a pumpkin. Let's go to Mr. J's."

I couldn't get Lucille's dying face out of my head. Her black eyes haunted me yet I pushed out half a smile.

He took my hand and forced it into our secret handshake, which ended with a fist bump. Like superheroes, we smashed fists three times. Whenever we did this, it meant that we were invincible to whatever was happening around us. "It's good to be superheroes," Dad exclaimed.

I felt better. "Yes, it is."

Chapter 3
Alien Farmer

The family station wagon bottomed out as we pulled off Route 7 into Johnson Vegetable Grove. We walked through the twisting gravel parking lot. Our family had been coming to Mr. Johnson's since I was four years old. He had the best produce and always gave out free samples. As soon as he saw us, he waved and came right over with two paper cups of home-brewed apple cider. A grin widened on his overly lined face.

"Try it," Mr. Johnson said wheezily. "It's good."

"Hello to you, too" Dad said, shaking his hand.

I gulped. "Delicious."

"The aliens gave me the recipe, Johnny. That's why it's so good."

I nodded. "Still going with that story?"

He snapped both straps of his overalls against his chest. "Always," he said, a believable look in his eyes.

Mr. Johnson was an oddity in our little town called Whisper. At ninety-nine years of age, he was the oldest living farmer in the county. He had a tendency to make things up, but we all loved him anyway. Mr. Johnson's best story was the continuing saga of aliens visiting his farm every year. They always left behind gifts of giant fruits and vegetables. Then Mr. J put them on display.

I looked around. We were the only ones there. I crumpled up the cup and tossed it into a rusty garbage barrel. The wooden shelves around us were overstuffed with fruits and vegetables. A sign read "From Outer Space." On display: a gourd shaped like a big brain, a strawberry weighing at least twenty pounds, and an ear of corn that resembled a long sword. I reached for the corn sword.

"Don't!" Dad yelled, shaking his finger at me. He turned to Mr. Johnson, "Edgar, show us your best pumpkins."

Mr. J shook his head in disappointment. "I don't have any," he said. "Not one pumpkin grew this year. I don't understand why. Everything else did."

I gave him my sad-eye look. "Why didn't the pumpkins grow?"

"I don't know, Johnny. Ever since I was a little boy, Johnson's has had a pumpkin patch." He took off his faded floppy hat and scratched his head. "Until this year. The story about the pumpkin shortage was in the newspaper. It's big 1960s news for our town. It was late August when the news hit, and now it's October. Didn't you guys read about it?"

"No, Mr. Johnson, must have missed that one," Dad said.

"Sounds kind of fishy, Mr. J," I added, with a shrug and my hands on my hips. "If that's true, you must have framed that newspaper. It goes well with your alien story. Can I see the newspaper?"

He shook his head. "I don't save any of my papers. After I read them, I use them in the hen house to control chicken poop." Mr. J picked a booger from his nose and flicked it.

I looked down, slapped my forehead and tried not to laugh. I was kind of mad, though, and my face showed it. Halloween was just a few days away. Time was running out.

Mr. Johnson patted me on the head, luckily not with his booger finger. "I'd be upset, too. Tap my fist. I've got something for you." He pulled something out of the pocket of his overalls and opened his hand.

"What is it?"

"It's a rainbow Peewee. My lucky marble. I want you to have it. Now it's your lucky marble. It's very old, from the 1800s."

"Cool!" I exclaimed happily. I rolled the marble back and forth across my palm. "Thanks, Mr. J."

Dad straightened the knot on his tie and winked at me. "We'll try another farm. There's a pumpkin out there for us." Before leaving, he bought a half-gallon of apple cider. I tucked the marble away in the front pocket of my cargo pants for safekeeping. We waved goodbye and drove down the road.

Chapter 4
The Bats

"Johnny, there's another farm at the end of this road. It's where Junction 66 and the railroad tracks cross. It's called The Cobblers. I heard a lot of good things about the old woman named Noel who runs the farm. Did you know she sells the best corn in all the land?"

"I didn't know that, Dad." I patted my stomach. "I love corn. Corn on the cob, corn fritters, corn dumplings, corn giblets."

"Stop, you're making me hungry."

I jumped in my seat. "Did you say her name is Noel?"

"Yeah, why?"

"I heard about her place from Jimmy. Tell Noel that you want to buy her pumpkin cane."

"She has a pumpkin cane? Hmm … she must be a hardcore fan of Halloween like you."

"There's more to the story than that. The cane has magic powers. Jimmy and some of our friends were playing Captain Maze in her cornfield just last week. They saw her doing something amazing!"

Dad looked puzzled. "Captain Maze, what's that?"

"It's like hide and seek. The best part is when you become the Corn King."

"Corn King! Now that's funny."

"She was picking corn, barrels and barrels of it. But she wasn't using her hands. She tapped the ears of corn with her cane, and one by one they jumped off their stalks into the bucket."

"Are you serious?"

"Jimmy swore to it. After we have the pumpkin cane, ha ha … we can run around all day and cast spells!"

Dad took one hand off the wheel to bop me on the head. "You and your wizards, boy, or should I say in this case a witch?"

"It has been a day of witches. I wonder if …."

"Don't even say it." Dad reached into his jacket pocket. He took out some lip balm and dabbed his lips.

House after house and field after field rolled by. With the wind in my face, I kept the window down while I spaced out staring at the autumn leaves and dreaming of the perfect Halloween adventure. Dad kept flipping the radio stations from talk radio to rock and roll. It was annoying, but I didn't say anything. Instead my eyes flickered, and I dozed off.

Sometime later Dad tapped my shoulder, "Come on, sleepyhead. We're here."

Noel's farm reminded me of a framed photo hanging in our living room. They both featured cows and horses, rows and rows of cornfields, a little dirt road, and a white paint-chipped house with brown shutters.

"What's that?" I asked as I pointed to a cylinder-shaped, stone structure taller than the roof of the house.

"It's called a silo. Farmers use it to store livestock feed." He looked around. "Now, where is that old woman?"

As I walked, I took out a lollipop and popped it into my mouth. The strawberry flavor was sweet and juicy. "I think I see her. Is that her on the porch in the rocking chair?"

"Call her name and see what happens."

I waved and shouted: "Hi, Noel!"

She shouted back, "Hi boys!" She walked hunched over and leaning on a curved wooden cane with a silver jack-o'-lantern for a handle.

I nudged Dad. "Look! She has the pumpkin cane."

She wore a leaf-covered embroidered sweater and a long black skirt. Her eyes looked crossed under her granny glasses. A puffy platinum blond wig flowed down her back. She had so much makeup on that she reminded me of a circus clown. Dad winked at her. "Hello, Noel. Do you have any pumpkins?"

A fly landed on her nose, and she smacked it with her hand. I watched the fly fall to the ground, still alive with a broken wing. I stomped it into the dirt. She pointed her cane at me then spoke in a low, creepy voice that cracked up and down with every syllable. "That would have been mighty tasty for my iguana, Cleopatra," she said. "She's in the kitchen in the cupboard."

I laughed so hard my sides began to ache. Dad gave me one of his famous stop-it looks. She continued on. With every word, her voice became more frightening. "Pumpkins? No one in Whisper does. In fact, I don't think any towns around these parts have any this year."

"What about your cane? It has a jack-o'-lantern on it. Dad told me, he wants to buy it."

"Johnny, I didn't say that."

She tapped the cane against the ground three times, and raging flames appeared in the jack-o'-lantern's eyes. "Young boy, it's not for sale. It's magic."

I nudged Dad and whispered to him, "Did you see that?"

He whispered back, "Yeah, I did."

I didn't want my favorite holiday to be ruined. I had to know why no one had pumpkins.

"Noel, why don't you have pumpkins?" I threw up my hands. "No one has pumpkins!"

Dad gave me his stop-it look again.

Noel crookedly smiled at me. "Bats. Fruit bats. Thousands of them. They came from the sky and ate all the pumpkin seeds across the land. My sister predicted the bats would come this year. She even gave me this pumpkin cane as a gift before it happened. I didn't believe her, until one dark night, in early May, I was looking out my window, and there they were digging in the garden."

Dad exclaimed, "What?"

Noel's eyes began to glow with raging flames for only a second. "Did you know that my sister is a grand witch? You must know. Everyone in town knows. She's been casting spells ever since the day her children died twenty years ago. She told me the bats would take the seeds to the place of dead spirits. That was the last thing she told me before she disappeared."

Dad raised his voice, "That's enough, woman!"

"You're Lucille's sister!" I probably shouldn't have said that.

The old woman's ears sprang up magically from under her wig. "You've seen her. Where did you see her? I've been looking ... trying so hard to find her. If you know anything about where she is, please, tell me!"

I didn't know what to say. It was too late to take back my words. I knew her sister was dead, but I didn't have the heart to tell her. Dad and I looked at each other then back at Noel. "We don't know where she is," we said in unison, shaking our heads.

"Boys, do not play games with me. You just said you knew Lucille. Tell me where she is, or I'm going to hit you with my cane!"

"You can't talk to us like that! We are out of here!" said Dad with clenched teeth.

Noel's friendly old lady appearance had disappeared. She whacked Dad over the head with the pumpkin cane. Blood leaked down his forehead.

"What the hell?" he asked. He pushed her, and she fell over.

I couldn't believe my eyes. *Why did I have to open my stupid mouth?*

At first we were walking then sprinting and now running. It was incredible. My Dad, my hero, was letting an old woman with a swinging pumpkin cane chase us to our car. I wondered how she could run that fast- as if she had superpowers. I wondered if the pumpkin cane was giving her superpowers.

She kept shouting: "Boys, tell me about my sister! You seem to know my sister!"

I jumped in the car as fast as I could. But dad wasn't as lucky. Noel caught up to him and whacked him in the back. With that, Dad couldn't control himself. He turned around, grabbed her by the arms, and tossed her at least ten feet. I knew Dad was strong, but I didn't know he was that strong.

I unlocked the car door for Dad, and he got in. He started up the engine. We were almost off, but that old woman shattered the back window with her cane. Through the chunks of flying glass, I glimpsed the flaming eyes of the jack-o'-lantern again. And then it started opening and closing its mouth, laughing at us horrifically. *Ha ha ha ha ha ha!*

We sped away, leaving that crazy woman in a cloud of exhaust.

"Eat our dust, you old bitch!" Dad shouted.

I looked in the side mirror and saw her still chasing us, swinging her pumpkin cane.

"What the hell just happened?"

"I don't know, Dad. We are having the worst day I think two guys could ever have."

"Johnny, why did you open your mouth about Lucille?"

"I'm sorry. I didn't know that would happen."

Dad wiped the blood off his forehead with a handkerchief. "It's okay, it's not your fault. That woman is nuts."

"Do you think we should tell the sheriff what happened?"

"Johnny, do you think I'm going to tell Kennedy that I got beat up by an old lady with a pumpkin cane? He would never believe me."

"I agree. The sheriff is stubborn. I was right about the two ladies knowing each other. Can you believe they're witch sisters?"

Dad looked nervous. "I believe this is not good."

"What are you going to tell mom about the back window of the car?"

"I'll tell her a tree branch shattered it. She doesn't have to know the truth. If we spill the beans about a dead witch, her crazy witch sister, bats eating pumpkin seeds, dead spirits, and dead kids your mom would be tough to live with for a while. She wouldn't sleep for months, maybe years. She probably wouldn't even let you go out and trick or treat on Halloween."

"What? No way!"

"I want you to remember, Johnny, you became a man today. Don't say anything to mom. Promise?"

We smashed fists.

"Yeah, I promise." I was good at keeping secrets. "Dad, there is just one thing I don't understand. Are you sure we shouldn't tell the sheriff?"

"I will, Johnny, in time."

"Why are you waiting? We should tell him now! Things are getting scary in our town."

"I have to get all the facts straight in my head. Then I will. I promise."

We smashed fists again.

Chapter 5
A Day In school

It was a school day that should have been like any other, but it wasn't. I was sitting at my desk drawing pictures of clowns in my English notebook and continuously staring at the clock on the wall. I wasn't paying attention to school at all. The idea of no pumpkins for Halloween kept flashing in my brain. I couldn't stop thinking about Lucille. Whenever I closed my eyes, I saw her dead in the road. I wondered about her sister Noel and her pumpkin cane. She attacked us. *Why wouldn't Dad tell the sheriff what happened? And why is he always hiding something?* I think my father is a villain. I'm not sure how I feel about that. It's time to get my brothers together for an investigation.

My mind drifted back to school. I was looking forward to the kickball game at recess. I was waiting for my turn to write a word on the blackboard for the spelling bee. My best friend Jimmy was up there with his hand curled around the chalk. He was trying to spell "opulent." He was stuck on one letter. My other best friend, Jay, sat next to me in the front row. He had his hand cupped over his mouth. When the teacher looked away, he whispered the missing letter.

I had been friends with Jimmy and Jay for many years. I called them my brothers. Jimmy lived across the street. He was shy, brainy, and cool. He liked fishing. We'd always go to Bow's Pond to catch catfish. We built a tree fort together in my back woods. Jay lived behind those woods. He was mechanical. He liked go-Karts and was really good at catching living creatures, especially snakes. We were four years old when we all became friends. We were like The Three Musketeers.

"No cheating!" the teacher yelled.

Sister Virginia was our teacher. She was short, heavy and German. The odd thing about her: she had a chicken neck. My friends and I would gobble like chickens sometimes, and she never knew why. Sister Virginia had really long, gray hair that no one ever saw down. It was always tied up in a bun, which reminded me of a beehive. She regularly kept a pencil inside the hive. During class she would take the pencil out all the time and use it as a pointer.

I knew Jimmy was in trouble because Samantha was across from him in the process of spelling "judgment." She was a major distraction due to the fact that she was the prettiest girl in the sixth grade. There was something about her. You fell into her eyes, and her smile stayed with you. She always wore hair bonnets. My friends and I were her slaves. We'd do anything for just one word from her.

The teacher had pitted the boys against the girls today. We were losing. They were two words up on us. "You're disqualified. Point to the girls. Thanks to your friend, you can sit down now, Jimmy," Sister Virginia said.

I attended Catholic school. Everyone was required to wear a uniform. My grade wasn't actually situated in the school. There wasn't enough room in the building for all the grades, so sixth was always housed outside in a large trailer. The nuns were cool overall, except when they got out the ruler. Knuckles presented then whack! I hadn't been hit this year, which was great for me because I was always getting into trouble. The last time I got hit I was almost out of fifth grade. I had decided to tie Sister Virginia's shoelaces together. Bad idea. My knuckles bled badly that day. I couldn't believe my bad luck. I got Sister Virginia again for a teacher. She had moved from fifth grade to sixth!

"Johnny, your turn," Sister Virginia said, tapping her pencil against my desk.

I made my way past the desks, and up the center aisle to the blackboard. A powerful breeze came through the window. The wind did no damage to my spiked hair, but it did get my attention. I stopped to stare out the window. A sky full of black storm clouds rolled over the sun. The day turned to night almost instantly. I took two more steps then froze when a loud explosion echoed from outside. It was the loudest thunder I'd ever heard. *Boom! Boom! Kaboom!*

"Sister Virginia, the sun is gone!" I shouted, gesturing toward the window. "Quick, everyone to the window!"

All my classmates ran to the window. Sister Virginia did not look happy about the ruckus I was causing. "Everyone calm down. Back to your seats. It's only a storm. We will continue with the spelling bee. This will take our minds off the storm," she said with a sneer.

"Bad idea, Sister Virginia," I responded. I grabbed her hand, and pulled her close to the window. She started watching with us.

The sky began to howl like a pack of wolves let loose upon the town. A light show began that reminded me of fireworks. Long bolts of lightning slammed into the ground. It began to rain, but this was no ordinary rain. The raindrops pounded the trailer like an army of hammers. The wind blew into the room again, but this time it splashed everyone with water and pushed us back. Kids screamed. When the wind settled down, Jimmy and I closed the window.

"Everyone under your desks!" Sister Virginia yelled, recognizing the danger.

We ran but not in time. The trailer shook violently before lifting off the ground and rising higher and higher into the air. It was The Wizard of Oz time! How high we went, I wasn't sure. I felt my stomach drop out from under me when we plummeted like a carnival ride into the ground. My classmates, the teacher, the desks, the blackboard, and everything else collided. The windows exploded upon impact. The trailer had landed on its side. Everyone was entangled like a treacherous game of Twister.

I pushed the desk off that had pinned me to the floor. The sleeve of my sweatshirt was torn, and I had a bruised arm. I looked around for my friends. "My brothers, where are you?" I shouted.

"Get off of me!" Jimmy yelled, as he rolled fat Marco into the bookshelf. They had smashed heads. "Ow! I'm over here." Jimmy rubbed the side of his head.

"I'm here," Jay answered. He was in a daze lying on the blackboard, which had cracked in half.

Everyone was yelling and screaming and crying. The teacher was trying to gather her strength by the starry look in her eyes. She had a nasty cut on her head. Trying to stop the blood from leaking down her face, she pressed the cut repeatedly with her hand. She then wrapped the wound with a hunk of paper and masking tape because the corner closet, which stored the bandages, was smashed up. She began to help my classmates to their feet. Everyone looked okay except for some scrapes and bruises.

I looked through a window shattered with spider-web cracks. A bright glow shined through the corner of it. Had the sun returned? How? What kind of storm could last for a few minutes and then completely disappear? I wondered if it could have been a tornado.

I lifted my head high and turned to my brothers. "So what do you think?"

"I'm up for an adventure," Jay responded with raised eyebrows. "Yeah! We should go check out the damage," said Jimmy. The three of us kicked the rest of the glass out of the window. Then one by one we crawled out.

"Boys! Boys! You should be helping your classmates! Where are you going?" Sister Virginia shouted. She turned to Abigail, Samantha, Tommy, Paul, and Stephen. "Help your friends," she told them. "I'll be back in a minute. I'm going to get them. Boys! Come back!"

I was the last one out. I never saw a nun run before, but she was coming at me. Maybe it was the shoelace thing. Maybe she was still upset. I don't think you could ever forget something like that. She grabbed my wrist and tried to pull me back. "She's got me, guys, help!" I shouted.

My brothers grabbed my other arm and pulled me in the opposite direction. They were having a tug of war with me! I hoped my brothers would win. I fell into the grass. I heard Sister Virginia's body slump to the ground. "Ouch, that hurt!" she shouted. Then I heard crying. "I'm gonna get you, Johnny Black!"

I couldn't believe it. Maybe she was disoriented because she kept following us. What was she thinking? She left all of those hurt kids behind. The sun sank as quickly as it had come back. The sky was turning black again. The trees around us blew like flowers in the wind. The windows and doors of the school rattled. The cross on the roof spun like a coin.

"Is this the eye of the storm?" Jay asked.

"Not anymore," Jimmy answered. "Would you look at that? Two of the cars in the parking lot are flipped over. Maybe we should go back."

"What are you, a wimp? It's balls to the wall out here." Jay flared his nostrils to sniff the air. "We like it like that."

Jimmy slapped Jay's hand. "I just needed a push."

I waved my brothers forward. "Come on, this way. Do you hear that?" I asked.

"What is that?" they both responded.

"Same time-zees," Jimmy said. He punched Jay in the arm and laughed.

"Where's Sister Virginia?" I asked them. We all turned around. She was treading toward us.

Jay waved to her. He shouted at the top of his lungs: "Go home! Nuns have no fun! Go home!"

"I'm going to get all of you!" she shouted back with her fists shaking in the air.

"Forget about her," I said. She's just another townsperson who's lost her mind."

"What do you mean by that?" Jay asked.

"I will tell you guys later. Come on. Let's find out what's making that strange bell sound," I said, tightening the drawstring of my hooded sweatshirt.

"It's so loud. Maybe it's Santa Claus," Jimmy offered.

"Wrong holiday," I corrected him.

"Probably church bells," said Jay, curling his hands inside the sleeves of his shirt.

"Let's see anyway," I added.

The transformation back to a pitch-black sky was done. The mighty thunder returned with the heavy rain that tried to pound us into the ground. We ran across the muddy grass to the white oak tree along Emperor Street. The tree was almost as tall as a skyscraper– more than twenty feet in circumference and having the thickest roots. The prize of Whisper, it was 350 years old, maybe more. Its giant leaves made a nice blanket against the newly falling hailstones.

"Better grab a branch, brothers," I suggested starting to climb.

Sister Virginia was trying her hardest to fight the wrath of the storm as she ran through the windy rain toward us. The sanctuary of the tree was less than a 100 feet away. The wind had freed her hair for the first time ever. It kept whipping her in the face. I questioned myself. *Why hadn't she gone back? She should have gone back.*

Squinting her eyes, she held her hand up and called out to us. "Children! We have to go in now!"

"Sister Virginia! Run faster!" I shouted.

"Oh my God!" Jimmy yelled, his hair soaked and blocking his eyes. The wicked wind knocked us around. Rocks and dirt spat into our faces. We held onto our branches for our dear lives. Mine was the strongest thing I'd ever felt.

Jay cried out, "Look at Sister Virginia!" She was being tossed into the air like a Raggedy Ann doll. Her arms and legs flopped as she splashed into the ground on her belly. Suddenly, the wind subsided. We jumped out of the tree onto the ground. The storm was gone as if it had never happened. The blinding sun popped up out of nowhere. We gathered around Sister Virginia. "Do you think she's okay?" Jay said, shaking water from his hair and ears.

"Let's flip her over," I suggested.

"Wow … she's heavy," said Jimmy.

"Like 200 pounds," Jay grunted.

We turned her over. "I don't think she looks so good," Jimmy commented.

"She'll be okay. She has to be." I changed subjects. I had to fill them in on what else was happening in our little town of Whisper. "My brothers ... I have to talk to you. I didn't get the chance to earlier. Yesterday dad and I met an old woman who died in front of us. I don't think I can handle someone else dying today."

Jay looked concerned. "Who died?"

"And what happened?" Jimmy asked.

"It was the craziest thing I ever saw. Dad and I were on our way to get a pumpkin and this lady in a muddy nightgown was laying face down in the street. She turned over and told us 'my boys are coming home' then she died. Her name was Lucille Bibimtaff."

"Why you messing with us Johnny?"

"I'm not messing with you Jimmy."

Jay pondered. "What did Lucille mean by what she said? And where do I know that name?"

"I think she was talking about her sons coming home."

"Where they coming home from Johnny?" Jimmy asked.

"Would both of you shut up and let me finish," I pleaded. "There is something really weird going on in Whisper? Not only did that woman die, but what about the pumpkins?"

Jay chewed a piece of bubble gum. He spoke in between chomps. "Didn't you hear? The pumpkin shortage story was in the newspaper. Those science people said all the seeds went bad this year. Blamed it on osmosis or something like that. The bottom line is this: no pumpkins for Halloween this year."

Jimmy flicked two fingers at Jay. "Osmosis. I think you got your reason mixed up."

"Will you guys let me talk? I thought Farmer Johnson made the whole pumpkin story up. There's something else. Remember Farmer Noel?"

"Holy shit JB! That's where I know that name from. Lucille is farmer Noel's sister. And yeah, we play Captain Maze all the time in her cornfield. She's so senile, she never knows we're there. I like her new pumpkin cane– so cool, that magic cane," Jay said.

"That little old woman attacked Dad and me yesterday with that cane. Did you know the jack-o'-lantern head on the cane glows? The cane laughed at us as she broke the back window of our station wagon with it. Noel's a witch. She looked like one and talked like one. All she was missing was her hat and broomstick."

"I'm surprised. You, Jay?" Jimmy turned to his friend.

"A laughing ... magic ... pumpkin cane. I could see that. Saw her do that corn trick with it. Couldn't figure out for a million bucks how she did it. I thought Noel was harmless. As far as her being a witch ... she could be," Jay replied.

"Did you ever meet her sister, Lucille?" I asked.

"No, who is she?" asked Jimmy.

"She's the one who caused the pumpkin shortage."

"How did she do that?"

"Black magic. She's also a witch. She's the woman I saw die yesterday. She's been searching for her dead kids for, like, twenty years or sixty years or something."

My brothers looked at me all creepy—like. "What?!" they both exclaimed.

Jimmy made a thumb gesture toward Sister Virginia. "Should we be talking like this in front of her?"

Jay slapped him on the shoulder. "Don't worry about her. She's seeing stars right now." He pushed her with his foot. She didn't move at all. "See?"

"Bottom line ... her sons were killed. She was very upset about their deaths before she died. I keep thinking about what her sister Noel said. How the bats took the pumpkin seeds to the place of dead spirits. Maybe she used the bats and the pumpkin seeds to bring someone back from the dead. Like her boys."

"How many boys we talking about?" Jay asked.

"Three."

"You guys are crazy. You can't raise someone from the dead. Sounds to me like you're ready for the white room, JB. You too, Jay, for just believing what he's saying."

I looked down at poor Sister Virginia. "There's something unbelievably wrong here. I say tomorrow after school we go talk to the sheriff and see what he knows about Noel. Are you guys up for a really dangerous adventure?"

"Maybe we could break into Noel's house and steal her pumpkin cane! See if it's really made of magic. I want to find out how it laughs. What do you think?" Jay asked, hopefully.
"No!" I shouted. "We start with the sheriff."

Jay and Jimmy reluctantly agreed.

Chapter 6
Storm Riders

I hoped the storm surges were finally over. The bell sound we were in search of was now louder than ever. Clang clang clang was all we heard over and over again. My friends and I froze with open mouths as we saw a horse-driven wagon with three riders who looked like carnival clowns approach us from over the hill. I wondered if the storm had conjured them.

Jimmy was on pins and needles. "Maybe we should hide. What if this thing came from hell?"

"Are you serious? They're clowns," I assured him.

Jimmy looked around for a safe place. "The bushes. We could hide behind the bushes."

"You hide. I'm staying."

"Me too," Jay said.

The clown sitting in the middle whipped the two black horses as they rode closer. I found it amazing that the wagon carried a giant cargo of bouncing pumpkins. How did they know we needed pumpkins? The top of the carriage read "ARNIVAL" in burned wooden letters. Broken metal chains dangled and smashed against the back of the wagon and dragged along the road.

Jimmy finally came to his senses. "Fine. I'll stand with you."

The clown driver pulled up on the reins. The horses neighed and slowed their trot to a halt. One clown stood up. He threw his arms and hands into the air. He shouted, "Ahhh!!! What a ride!" This clown looked very short. Could he be a midget? Were my brothers and I about to be visited by midget clowns?

The clown next to him spoke. "I didn't think we would make it through the lightning, but the thunder was music to my ears. What happened to moth—?"

The third clown waved him to stop. He pointed at us. "Enough! They're watching."

My brothers and I stood there in shock. Who were these clowns? What were they doing in Whisper? "Did anyone hear about a carnival coming to town?"

"Did he just ask him what happened to a moth?"

"I think so, Jay" Jimmy answered.

Jay clapped his hands together. It was to break up tension he was feeling. "The only carnival I know about is the graveyard."

I was confused. "Huh?"

"That's what we call what's left of the Ferris wheel behind the railroad tracks. Jimmy, remember when you and I climbed to the top of the broken Ferris wheel?"

"I remember. That Ferris wheel is at least fifty feet high. You fell, luckily into the bucket seat below. I can still see you swinging. If I hadn't pulled you up, you wouldn't be here today."

Jay put out his fist in gratitude. Jimmy smashed his fist against his own. "Brothers for life. That was cuckoo crazy."

"Brothers, how come you never invited me there?"

"I guess you were never around when we went. It's still there if you want to see it."

"I have to see the Ferris wheel but not now." I gestured with my head toward the clowns.

"We got other things going on." One by one the clowns climbed down from the wagon. The bells on their red and black floppy hats jingled. I realized they were not midgets. They were boys around our age. I wondered if they could be Lucille's sons raised from the dead. I whispered to my brothers, "I think it's them."

Jimmy was a non-believer. "It's not them," he stated flatly.

On the other hand, Jay was more open minded. "Holy shit, JB! What if you are right?"

I whispered again, "Let's keep this to ourselves until we figure out what is going on."

We studied the clowns closely. Their faces were painted bright white with black bats around their beady black eyes. They each had three red tears painted under their right eyes. Round red rubber noses and black smeared lipstick completed their farcical faces. Their polka-dot shirts, pants, and big floppy shoes with giant tongues were covered in splattered mud.

Jimmy said what was on his mind. "Death clowns who've come to kill us for what we've done to Sister Virginia, making her chase us like that."

"Jimmy, stop it. All clowns are friendly. Most likely they came here to put on a show." My brothers and I lined up as if we were about to have a showdown with the clowns. One laughed in a deep, dark voice. "Ha ha ha ha ha ha." His laughter sounded familiar. It brought me back to Noel shattering the back window of the station wagon with the laughing pumpkin cane.

"I'm ready to run," Jimmy said.

"You know it, brother. Time to go, JB." I closed my eyes and prayed for something to save us. Jay nudged me in the side. "Johnny, look!"

Everyone in the school stood behind us. They were as fascinated and horrified as we were. Some of the nuns gathered around Sister Virginia. They were praying and trying to wake her up. Fat Marco stood behind me with his bent glasses and torn corduroy shirt. He appeared to be nervous as hell. I could feel his sweat spraying across my back. I turned to glare at him. "Control yourself," I said.

He was trembling with tears in his eyes. "I don't like clowns. They give me nightmares." He pointed at the clowns. "What happened to your fingers? Why are you all missing fingers?"

Why didn't I notice the clowns had stumps for some of their fingers? Why didn't my brothers notice? The clowns wiggled their hands, waving at everyone with the few fingers they had. A lot of kids and nuns started screaming. My heart was pounding really fast. I could feel everyone's fear closing in on me. My words skipped. "Wh–wha–what do you want?"

"Trick or treat?" they asked together. They waved to us again. All their fingers were whole this time. "Welcome to the haunted Halloween show. We are traveling Halloween clowns." They all bowed.

It was magic. Oh my God! *It was magic*. I squeezed my hands against Jimmy and Jay's shoulders. I felt so relieved and started laughing. Everyone was laughing. Marco was even laughing. One clown came forward. I think he was the boss. "My friends, the name is Patches," he said calmly.

"Why you're no bigger than me," Jay observed, as he played with the peace symbol pendant around his neck.

"That's right," Patches replied.

"How come you're all dirty?" Jimmy asked.

"The storm. We traveled through the worst of it."

The clown next to Patches grinned then spoke in a high-pitched crackly voice. "Sebastian is the name. I like this place. Have any of you eaten worms? Have you ever been stoned? Did you ever see the winged D—?"

"Sebastian!" the last clown yelled, cutting him off. "Stop your chatter. It hurts people."

Most of my classmates' faces turned ghostly white. Whoever was laughing wasn't laughing anymore. "Why do you keep trying to scare us?" I asked.

"It's part of the magic show. My name is Aloysius."

"Well, get on with it," Jay said impatiently. "You clowns are little. I think all of us could take you."

I nudged Jay. "Stop it!"

Jimmy took control of the crowd by shouting as loud as he could. "Everybody let's go home! These aren't real clowns. If they were, we'd be laughing. Look at Samantha. She's crying."

One kid shouted back: "He's right! We should go!"

From the distance, one Sister chimed in, "Go away, clowns. Go entertain someone else. Someone please tell me an ambulance has been called for Sister Virginia?"

Patches was not pleased. "You don't want the haunted Halloween show?"

"No!" everyone shouted.

But he would not take no for an answer. "Magic awaits. Let the show begin!" He levitated a few feet off the ground. "We are just children like a lot of you but also great magicians," he boasted, hovering on the air as if he had superpowers. Out of Patches' pocket flew a bat then another one and another. The winged beasts flew over to Sebastian picked him up and dropped him into the pile of pumpkins. As he crashed the bats vanished. My classmates and the nuns went crazy with laughter and hand clapping.

Sebastian began to throw pumpkins to Aloysius. Aloysius caught all three and juggled them. I couldn't believe my eyes when they then transformed into balls of flames.

I saw Sister Mary out of the corner of my eye. She must have been the last one to leave the school because everybody else was here.

She ran toward Patches and waved her hand. In her other hand she tightly held onto her rosary beads. She shouted, "Stop! Stop! Stop! Are you blind? My best friend is dying over there!"

Aloysius threw burning pumpkins at her as she trembled in fear. The pumpkins disappeared into puffs of smoke upon impact. Her voice turned brittle: "What's wrong with you people? Evil children!" She shook her head in disgust.

"It's only magic," Patches said with a sinister smile. He moved away from her to stroke leaves of the old oak tree. Then he jumped back onto the ground and stood before Sister Mary.

She towered over him with shaking hands. "Who are you?" The bridge of her nose crinkled. "Why are you here?"

Patches cupped her hands into his and pressed the cross of the rosary beads. He hugged her. She reluctantly accepted the embrace. "No harm, lady. I grieve for your loss," Patches said disingenuously.

She looked over at Sister Virginia. "What do you mean?"

The nuns were still praying. They opened their eyes when one Sister stated in an unsettled voice, "I'm afraid to say Sister Virginia has left us."

"I'm sorry," Patches said.

Sister Mary screamed, "No, you're not!" She squirmed out of his hold.

I felt sad. My teacher was dead.

At that moment a rosebud appeared in Sister Mary's hand. It was glowing as if on fire.

She held it to her nose and inhaled, sighing happily. She began to dance around like a ballerina on her recital day. Round and round she spun.

"Mary! What are you doing?" several nuns shouted in unison from the distance.

She threw the fiery rose into the grass then stomped it into oblivion. Her eyes turned mean and her fists clenched. "My best friend is dead!" she yelled, running down the street until she was out of sight. Madness overcame the horses. With loud snarls, they pulled against their harnesses, trying to break them. The wagon bucked into the air. As it crashed down, the gate opened. All the pumpkins spilled out and rolled toward us. I grabbed one. My friends did the same. Soon almost everyone held a pumpkin in his or her arms.

Sebastian closed the gate to the empty wagon. He nodded his head. "You ready?"

Patches loudly replied, "Wait!" He looked around with an amused expression on his face. "Keep the pumpkins," he told us. "We heard you had none. It's our way of saying thanks for watching our magic show."

We all cheered.

The clowns climbed up into the wagon, cracked a whip, and disappeared down the road. It was as if they vanished into a ball of dust. Soon the sheriff arrived. He was surprised to see me again. "Hello, Sheriff," I said.

"What happened, Slim?"

"The storm killed Sister Virginia then these clowns came. They put on a magic show and gave us pumpkins."

"I'm carving mine tonight," Jimmy interjected.

"Me too," Jay agreed.

"Are you guys for real?" asked the sheriff.

"It's weird, Sheriff, but it's true," I assured him.

The Sisters backed up our story.

"All right, everyone go back to the school and take your pumpkins with you. Nothing more to see here."

"Sheriff, shouldn't you keep the pumpkins as evidence?" I asked.

"You, your friends, and the nuns just told me the storm killed Sister Virginia. Why would I fill my squad car with pumpkins?"

I cupped my hand around my mouth and whispered to the sheriff so no one else could here. "I can't tell you in front of all these people."

"Slim, do you want me to call your dad?" the sheriff whispered back.

"No, I just need to talk to you."

"Okay, Johnny. You can stay. Everyone else, clear out! Don't forget your pumpkins. Halloween is just a few days away. I want to see some nicely carved Jack-o'-lanterns on everyone's porches."

"Sheriff, I don't think that's a good idea." He looked at me quizzically. "Everyone, listen to me!" I shouted. "Don't take the pumpkins! I have an awful feeling something bad will happen!"

"J.B., what the hell, man? I'm taking my pumpkin," Jay declared, clutching to his chest.

"Yeah, Johnny. What are you doing?" Jimmy asked.

The sheriff was getting mad. "Johnny, if you keep defying me like this I will arrest you," he said. I grumbled under my breath, visualizing myself behind bars. I definitely didn't want that. He waved everyone else away.

"What's up, Slim?"

"I think the Halloween clowns are Lucille's sons. I think she raised them from the dead."

The sheriff's scowl turned into a grin. "Lucille is dead. Even if she was alive you can't raise someone from the dead?"

"She cast her spell before she died," I explained.

"Damn! You have a wild imagination. I know I said Lucille was a witch, but you can't raise someone from the dead."

"I don't know how she did it, but it was like the clowns rode the storm into our world. Who knows where they came from? Maybe they broke out of hell! The wagon had broken chains dragging from the back of it.

The sheriff started laughing.

"Don't laugh. There's more. Dad and I went to Noel's farm to find a pumpkin. Of course she didn't have any. She told us about flying bats and how they ate all the pumpkin seeds in town. That's why the pumpkins never grew. The bats flew the seeds to the place of dead spirits. In case you didn't know, Noel is Lucille's sister. When we refused to tell her that her sister was dead, she attacked us with a laughing, magic pumpkin cane. She even broke the glass on the back of the station wagon."

"Why didn't you tell her?"

"We didn't want to hurt her feelings."

"Like I said, you have some imagination. Take your pumpkin and get out of here. I'm going to tell you like I told you before: Lucille is dead. It's over."

I put my head down in defeat. "Maybe you're right. Maybe my imagination is playing tricks on me."

"Of course I am. I'm the sheriff. I want to see the scariest pumpkin on your porch, Johnny."

"Okay." I took my pumpkin and walked back to the school. An ambulance with flashing lights passed me on its way to pick up my dead teacher.

Due to the death of Sister Virginia, school was closed until after her funeral. I couldn't escape the leash my mom had me on. I was grounded for venturing out into the storm.

Almost every kid in school went to the funeral. Everyone dressed in their gloomiest colors. We stood around under umbrellas with rain pouring down on us. It was burial time. My mom smiled at me with sad eyes as she gently massaged the back of my head. My Dad couldn't be there because of a lamp contract. He was in California taking care of business. Dad manufactured lamps for a living–lots of them. He felt bad about missing the funeral, but Sister Virginia died while he was away.

Father Michael gave himself communion after dedicating his prayer to Sister Virginia. He had been the priest of the Church of Saints for around thirty years. He dressed in a cape with gold fringe. A multi-colored steel cross dangled below his chest. He took off his square glasses, dropped them into his pocket, and held up the Holy Bible. "Sister Virginia is with Jesus now. She loved you, children. She donated her life to the Lord, our Savior. We are saying goodbye in the most special way today." Father Michael nodded.

Sister Virginia's decorated maple-wood casket was slowly lowered into the ground. Father Michael shoveled a pile of uncovered dirt next to the new grave on top of the coffin. "Now it's your turn," he said to Sister Mary.

She walked up to the grave, kissed her cross, and looked down. "I miss you. I bet you are having tea with God right now. I keep having the strangest dreams ever since that clown put that rose in my hand. I'm scared. What do I do, Virginia? Tell me what to do." She closed her eyes, folded her hands, and began to pray. Suddenly, she turned around and looked at everyone attending the funeral. She shouted, "The pumpkins! They are gifts from the devil. Destroy them before it's too late!"

Most people stood there with ghastly expressions on their faces. The rest laughed at her. "I want you to calm down," said Sister Helen as she approached.

"No! We have to stop them! They will kill us all!" Sister Mary shouted.

Father Michael and several Sisters gathered around Sister Mary with reaching hands.

"What do you mean, Sister Mary?" asked Father Michael with compassion.

Sister Mary didn't answer. She ducked and ran away from their reach. She tore through the cemetery shouting, "The devil's pumpkins are coming! The devil's pumpkins will live!"

I turned to my mother. "What if Sister Mary is right?"

"Do you really think Whisper will be invaded by monster pumpkins? That's crazy, son. You sure have some imagination. Sister Mary is obviously not well."

"I guess you are right. That's what the sheriff told me, too. When is Dad coming home?"

"He will be back from his trip, tonight. You will see him in the morning."

"Great!"

Father Michael seemed to have difficulty getting through the funeral, but he did it. We all paid our respects to Sister Virginia and went home.

Chapter 7
Halloween

Beep! Beep! Beep! I pounded my alarm clock button with my fist. I was excited. It was Halloween. My favorite holiday was here. I went downstairs and made myself a bowl of cereal then watched a cartoon called *Demon Land*.

I knew Dad was tired from his long business trip, but I wanted to wake him up early anyway. I had big plans with him. We always waited until Halloween to carve our pumpkin and buy my costume. Some people would say there would be no costumes left, but there always were. It was our family tradition.

I ran down the hall toward my parents' room. The hallway shook from my heavy feet. My Dad's favorite painting-showing the beginning of the mountain road-fell and broke. I knew he would be upset, so I hid the glass evidence behind the couch. Maybe he wouldn't notice for a few days. I didn't want to get grounded on Halloween. My parents were sleeping, so I jumped on the bed and began to dance around. Dad grabbed me and took me down. The covers sucked me in. "Go back to sleep, tiger," Dad moaned sleepily.

"Dad … Mom … get up!" I tugged on both of them. Mom held me in her arms. That was all it took. I slept with my parents for the next few hours.

When mom rose, she went to the grocery store. We needed more candy because Dad and

I had been snacking on Halloween chocolates for weeks. The pumpkin sat on the kitchen table. It was carving time. Dad had a knife in front of him and a black magic marker. I held up my chocolate milk. "A toast to the clowns who gave us this pumpkin."

Dad tapped his orange juice against my glass. "I'll drink to that."

I downed my entire glass of chocolate milk. "Delicious."

"Johnny, what happened that day?" he asked.

"It was the strangest thing I ever saw: except for our run-ins with Lucille and her sister Noel. I still have nightmares about both of them."

"Me too, son."

"Then there was Sister Mary when she freaked out at Sister Virginia's funeral. She told everyone that the pumpkins the clowns gave us would come alive and kill everyone in town. I don't want to scare you, Dad, but after we carve our pumpkin into a jack-o 'lantern it might come to life tonight and turn into a monster. It might break down the door and try to kill us."

Dad burst out laughing. He picked the pumpkin up and shook it. He held it to his ear.

"What are you doing?" I asked.

"I'm listening for the monster," he joked. He placed the pumpkin back on the table and laughed some more. I joined him in laughter. "Wow! That was funny," he said, tears in his eyes. "Now tell me about the clowns?"

"They arrived a few minutes after the storm ended. They rode over to us in a horse-drawn farm wagon called the Arnival. The wagon was filled with pumpkins."

"Stop right there! Arnival? Is that what you just said?"

"Yup, Arnival was the name."

Dad's face turned pale. He didn't look well. "Johnny, I just remembered. I have to make an important phone call for work."

"What about carving the pumpkin?"

"After I make my call, we will carve the best jack-o'-lantern in town." He left the room.

Who was he calling? Why now? I tried to follow him, but he went into his bedroom and closed the door. I listened with my ear pressed up against the door. That didn't work so I ran as fast as I could into the family room. I quietly picked up the phone. "I think the boys came home," Dad said.

"Don't worry", responded the sheriff. I recognized his voice. "It wasn't them."

"How do you know? You didn't see them."

"Your son told me about them. Those boys can't come back. They are dead."

"Did Johnny tell you about Arnival?"

There was a long pause. "I will look into the matter," the sheriff concluded. Click. The phone went silent.

I ran as fast as I could back to the kitchen. My head was spinning. I couldn't help but imagine that Dad and the sheriff killed the Bibimtaff brothers. I pictured a judge sentencing them to life in prison.

Dad seemed fine when he returned to the kitchen. "All right. It's carving time," he announced. He drew a face with slanted eyes and a mouth with a tongue. It made me laugh. He cut off the top of the pumpkin and scooped out the seeds. Then he cut out the face. There was no doubt in my mind that my Dad had carved the coolest jack-o'-lantern on the block. We put it on the front porch.

"Light it," I exclaimed.

"No. You know we always wait until dark. How about we go to the mall–find you a scary costume for tonight?" We hopped in the car and drove over. The Halloween Shop was decorated with ghouls, ghosts, and skeletons. The store was packed with people. I found the costume wall right away. It was almost empty.

My smile turned into a tight-lipped frown. "Can we go to the Party Store instead?" I asked Dad.

"No! I promised your ma we'd be back before five. Just pick one. I'll help you." Dad picked up a Grim Reaper costume and put it on. He grabbed a plastic sickle off the shelf and began to swing it around. He pretended to cut off my head.

"You're funny."

I noticed two of my classmates standing a few feet away. They were the tallest kids in school–brothers and identical twins, in fact. My friends and I called them "The Godzillas" because they would always fight with each other or anyone they felt like torturing. I remember hearing about how Tony Godzilla egged on Joey Godzilla last year at Trinity School to beat up their teacher. Joey walked up to old man

Samadi. "Hello, punk," he said. Then he punched him in the nose. They both got expelled. That's how they ended up at my school. Their father and mother were noted for saying over and over again how the nuns would straighten them out and make them good boys. But I had different thoughts about them. Evil comes to mind. The brothers always dressed the same to make it difficult to tell them apart. They switched classes all the time, and the nuns never knew. They had pointed ears, caterpillar eyebrows and mischievous eyes.

Today they wore matching jogging suits. Tony had a costume in his hand. He was arguing with his brother. "I saw it first, Joey. I'm going to be Lech. You will feel my wrath of spells," he said.

"No way! I'm the older one. I get to be the wizard," Joey retorted. He threw the first punch, knocking his brother into the spooky tee-shirt rack. It went flying to the floor. So did Tony. "You shouldn't have done that, Joey," Tony warned, getting his brother in a headlock. He was choking Joey whose face was turning red. "I'm going to kill you!" Tony shouted as Joey broke free. Both knocked over the wall of masks.

"They're like wild animals," Dad commented.

The Godzillas' mother appeared. I now understood why the brothers were so tall. Their mother was an Amazon. She grabbed them by the ears, dragging them to the front of the store. Tony dropped the Lech costume. I saw my chance and took it.

Halloween night came. While staring into our oval mirror, I put on my new costume. I saw myself as a great sorcerer. I adjusted my wizard hat, put on my necklace of ancient magic books, fastened my cloak, and waved my wand. "Take that!" I shouted as a lightning bolt burst out of the end of the wand, shot through the window, and blew up my neighbor's house.

My mom's voice returned me from fantasy back to reality. "Johnny, you almost ready?"

"Yeah, Ma. Be right there!" I went downstairs, and ran into Dad in the family room. I smacked him on the head with my wand. "Where's your costume?"

"I never dress up. You know that."

I shrugged my shoulders. "I know. I keep hoping one Halloween you will."

Dad flexed his upper body. "Lech, we meet again! I've heard of your magic. How you turn people into books."

I ran at him. He let me tackle him to the floor, and we wrestled. I could tell he was letting me win. We laughed strange until a foul stench entered the room. "What is that awful smell?" I asked.

"I think it's coming from the kitchen." We walked into the kitchen where Mom was cooking. Dad and I covered our noses. "Do you smell that horrible smell, dear?" Dad asked.

She sneezed. "I can't smell anything. I have a cold."

"Bless you," I said.

Buzzzzz. The timer went off. "Time for the surprise." She put on a pair of mitts, opened the oven, and pulled out a pan. She screamed.

Dad grabbed her hand. "What's wrong?"

"Look!" She pointed. All the pumpkin seeds in the pan had turned blood red. Each seed was pulsating like a little human heart. The stench was nearly unbearable. The seeds started exploding one by one like firecrackers. Smoke poured from the pan, quickly filling the kitchen. We all started coughing. Then the fire alarm went off.

Dad grabbed the pan and ran outside. We followed him to the front porch. He dropped the pan at the end of the driveway. Mom and I finally caught our breath and stopped coughing.

"Is everyone okay?" Dad yelled to us.

"We are all right!" We shouted in response.

"Good," he said. He went back inside to turn off the fire alarm then returned to embrace us. We stood together and watched the tray until there was no more smoke.

I finally took notice of other things around us. Our jack-o'-lantern was glowing perfectly. Our street was crawling with trick-or-treaters. I was excited. Soon I would be able to join in on the fun.

With a triumphant smile on his face Dad threw the pumpkin-seed pan into the garbage. "It was just a bad batch. Don't worry about it," he assured us.

I tapped him on the arm. "Uh, Dad, the garbage is on fire."

"Quick! Johnny, get the hose!"

I ran behind the house. By the time I returned to the front, water was spraying out of the nozzle. The garbage can, meanwhile, was fully engulfed. A few parents and children gathered around to watch, among them our neighbor Mr. Wolasul and his son. Jack was dressed up as Lech's archenemy The Sleep Fiend. He wore a long jacket covered in faces. A pouch of magic dust hung around his neck. If one speck of the dust touched your skin, your face would appear on his jacket. You could never go to sleep again.

Old lady McMullen looked on with her granddaughter Alina. I thought Alina looked so pretty as Jasmine the Seeress. She wore a crown of bird feathers in her hair. Her body fit tightly into a short-sleeved yellow sundress. She had golden bracelets on her wrists and a necklace of owls around her neck. The owls sometimes sprung to life to guide her toward visions of the future. Her job was to come to Lech's aid in the form of dreams.

I couldn't believe we all had dressed up as characters from *Demon Land*.

Dad yanked the hose from my hands and doused the flames.

Mr. Wolasul asked, "What happened?"

Old lady McMullen tipped her eyeglasses suspiciously. "We have the right to know."

"Grease fire," Dad exclaimed, shaking his head. "The fire is out. Everything is okay now. Why don't you take your kids up to the house? My wife will give them some candy."

"Nice costume, Johnny," Mr. Wolasul said with a grin. He and Jack walked away. Old lady McMullen and Alina followed. I tried to leave with them, but Dad stopped me. Alina waved goodbye.

As we walked back to the house, I asked: "Why did you lie? You didn't tell them."

"I couldn't. If I did, they would have thought I was crazy."

"You saw the pumpkin seeds. They looked like bloody beating hearts."

"No, they didn't. Your mom cooked them too long in the oven. That's why the seeds exploded."

"That's not true. Why are you lying again?" I probed.

"Don't talk to me like that! I'm your father. Do you not want to go trick or treating?"

"Dad, I can't stop thinking about all the crazy things happening to our town. What are we going to do to investigate?"

"I know what's best for you. We are going to do nothing. That's Kennedy's job. He's the sheriff, not us."

"Is there something you're not telling me? I need to know the truth."

"You know everything that I know. I would never lie to you, son."

I mumbled. "Yeah, you would."

"What did you say?"

"Nothing." I put my fist out, and Dad smashed it.

He smirked. "All right. Let's go trick or treating."

Chapter 8
Trick or Treat

Mom took a picture of Dad and me with our silly faces. She tossed a caramel into my pillow sack. "First one," she said.

I smiled. "I'm gonna fill the whole sack this year. Dad and I have the best route planned out."

"Let's go," Dad chirped.

Out into the street we ventured. We stopped at Mr. Flagstone's first. His porch light was on. I rang his doorbell. It was really cool. The sound of exploding bombs filled the air. Next came the sound of a loud plane's engine fading away. The door creaked open. Mr. Flagstone sat in his wheelchair with a big smile on his face.

"Trick or treat?" I asked.

"Johnny, you're a wizard. How nice," he said in a raspy voice.

Mr. Flagstone was a veteran of World War II. He always wore his hat with three medals dangling from it. One of them was the Purple Heart. Dad once told me that this award was the highest you could get for service to your country. Mr. Flagstone paid the price with his legs. I don't think it was such a good deal. He looked like Colonel Custer with his snow white, handle bar mustache, and long goatee. He was a loner. "Come in, boys," he said.

Dad would always tell me how Mr. Flagstone had a full wall collection of guns: I wanted to see it so bad badly.

A black and white photograph of a WWII fighter plane hung in the foyer. A tiger was painted on the front of the plane. Under the picture was an overgrown rubber tree. A tray with a giant bowl of candy was perched on top of the table next to the tree. "Here you go, kid," he said. He tossed two giant candy bars into my sack.

He was the only person on my street who gave out giant candy bars. I saluted him. "Thanks a lot, Colonel."

He saluted back. "You're welcome, Soldier."

"May I use your bathroom?" I asked, bravely.

"Johnny, why didn't you go at home?" asked Dad.

"I drank two pops. It's just hitting me now."

"Down the hall, to the right, first door," Mr. Flagstone, directed.

I really didn't have to go to the bathroom. I was in search of guns. Dad and Mr. Flagstone talked as I walked away. I didn't listen to anything they said. Walking left instead of right, I got lucky. I opened the door to the room of guns and stood there with my tongue on the floor. Indeed, the wall was covered, not just by new guns, but also by old guns dating back to the Civil War and even cowboy days. I knew this because we had studied some of these guns in class. I saw a musket, a six-shooter, a bayonet, a machine gun, a shelf full of grenades among many other weapons. More than half of the weapons I could not identify. I felt like a kid in a candy store. I imagined what it would be like to fire some of them. My eyes felt like they were bugging out when I spotted a bazooka. I didn't stay too long. I feared being caught.

"I like your jack-o'-lantern," Dad said as I returned from my search.

"Great detail in its sinister face," I added.

Mr. Flagstone put his hand up to his ear. "What did you say?"

"Your jack-o'-lantern!" Dad shouted.

"What about it?"

"We like it!" I yelled.

"Happy Halloween, boys." He closed the door.

We took the cobble stone path to a stone house and walked up to the wraparound front porch. I sat in the antique rocking chair under a dim light. I rocked as fast as I could. Under a haystack to the left of the door were not one, but three glowing jack-o'-lanterns. Halloween decorations depicting spider webs and creative faces adorned the windows. I rapped the gold lion-head knocker three times against the door. A little old lady appeared with a sweet smile. She reminded me of my grandmother. "Trick or treat," I said.

"Hello there, magic man," she said in a tiny voice.

A group of kids stood behind us in mostly monster costumes. The sweet old lady passed out licorice sticks. She even gave Dad a treat then went back inside. Two kids in masks approached me. One was dressed as the Terrible O and the other Poison Maker–

characters from Demon Land again. I couldn't get away from that show. "Hey, Lech, want to battle?" One asked. He raised his weapon, which was a blood-spattered black sword.

"You're no match for the wizard Lech." I waved my wand. "Ashes to ashes, return to nothing."

He dropped his sword and fell to the ground. "I'll poison you in the dark," the other one warned, raising a blue potion in his hand. I couldn't believe it when he actually opened the potion flask and threw the liquid at me.

"All right, guys," Dad interfered. "That's enough!"

We all started laughing. The two boys removed their masks. "What's up, Johnny B?" Jay asked. "You made plant food out of me."

"My poison will kill you in the next five seconds," Jimmy declared. I grabbed my throat and pretended I couldn't breathe. I don't know why, but Jimmy apologized to Dad. "Sorry about that, Mr. Black. We were just playing Demon Land."

"It's okay, Jimmy. I get it," Dad responded.

"You guys want to trick or treat with us?" I asked.

"I wouldn't want to ruin your father and son time," Jimmy answered.

Jay whispered to me with his hand cupped. "The brothers are slaving over Eva tonight. I wish you could join us."

I took a long glance at Eva. I had to after Jay said that. She looked real cute dressed up as a folk singer. She even had a guitar. I smiled while whispering back to Jay. "Me, too."

As we began to leave for the next house, a loud voice echoed across the night. Everyone froze in their footsteps. The voice sounded like a woman's. She was shouting at the top of her lungs, in an intense, blood-curdling pitch. "Someone is being eaten by the ghosts of Halloween. I love it!" Jay commented.

"She's so garbled. I can't make out what she is saying," Eva said.

"Someone is fooling around. It's definitely a Halloween prank," Dad offered.

Jimmy put his Poison Maker mask back on. "I don't hear the voice anymore."

Eva strummed a few notes on her guitar. "Let's get out of here."

The Terrible O pointed his sword toward the next house. "Follow me," he directed. I slapped his hand then the hand of the Poison Maker. After all it was Halloween, so no wacky voice in the night was going to stop them. The group of kids left. Dad and I were alone again.

The screaming voice returned. "Maybe someone needs help," I wondered.

"We should investigate the voice," Dad replied.

"Finally, you said the word 'investigate'. I like it."

We turned onto Crown Street. I couldn't believe my eyes when we saw Sister Mary running toward us. She was shouting at passing trick-or-treaters, "The devil's pumpkins are coming! The devil's pumpkins will live!"

"Dad, that's what she kept shouting at Sister Virginia's funeral. I'm worried for Mom. She's home alone."

"Nothing is going to happen to your mother. Come on, that's absurd. Sister Mary has lost her mind." It was clear that parents were now afraid of Sister Mary. We watched them scoop up their children and abandon the street. "Let's follow her," Dad suggested.

We shadowed Sister Mary to a house then hid behind some bushes so she couldn't see us. A teenage girl with dangling bug eyes and a New Year's Eve hat answered the door. She clenched a colored party popper between her teeth and blew it at Sister Mary. "Bless you, child," the nun responded.

The girl removed her glasses. "Sister Mary, what are you—"

Sister Mary placed her index finger against the girl's lips. "Shhh child. I have come to save you and your family."

"Do you remember me? I'm Maria. You used to be my fourth-grade teacher."

Sister Mary didn't answer the question. Instead, she picked up the glowing jack-o 'lantern from the porch and ran into the street with it. She dropped the jack-o 'lantern onto the pavement then jumped on it until the pumpkin turned into a pile of orange mush. She shouted at Maria: "Go, my child, go. Every pumpkin must be destroyed!

Maria stood there shaking her head. Dad and I approached. "What's wrong with Sister Mary?" she asked.

"Young lady, lock your door. Don't open it for anyone," Dad instructed. "Are your parents home?"

"They're watching Fright TV."

"Tell them what happened. Don't open your door for anyone. Good night," Dad said. We followed Sister Mary to the end of the street. She quickly drew an audience–people standing on their porches and some even sitting on the rooves of their houses. The people cheered as she stole their jack-o'-lanterns from right under their noses then bashed them on the pavement. "Halloween is over," Dad declared mournfully.

"Yeah ... get your paper ... the pumpkin-smashing nun." We were about to turn back onto Emperor Street when the sheriff's car drove past us with its bright lights beaming. Seeing Sister Mary, the sheriff turned on his siren. But she continued on her pumpkin-smashing warpath. The sheriff stopped. He and his deputy got out of their car with guns drawn. "What do you think?" I asked Dad, excitedly.

"Kennedy's here. Let him handle it. Let's go home. You are right. We should check on your mother."

Chapter 9
True Faces

As we walked back home, the wind began to howl like a great beast roaming the street. It started to rain. Loud thunder and lightning followed. The storm felt familiar. I had a bone-chilling fear the clowns would soon be here. "Do you hear the bells chiming?" I asked Dad.

"I do. What is that, tiger?"

"That's how it starts!"

"What starts?"

"They're coming!"

"Talk to me. Who's coming?"

I had to shout over the wind and bells. "The clowns!"

Our neighbor's roof suddenly began to disintegrate. It started with the shingles then the wooden planks. Pieces of the stone chimney broke off and floated upward with the swirling wind. The gathering tornado shredded the pieces into projectile missiles that bombed the street. Dad shouted, "Run!"

It was too late. We were thrown to the ground. Dad covered me with his body. I could hear voices laughing in the wind. The laughter grew louder and louder with each passing second. Dad cried out in pain when a brick fragment hit him in the back. A broken two-by-four shot like an arrow pierced the ground in front of us. Dad pulled me to my feet, and we ran like hell toward our house. I heard a loud crack. A telephone pole swayed then fell over onto Mr.

Wolasul's car, smashing it like a pancake into the road. The power lines snapped with sparks of electricity zapping the air. At that moment, the sky opened up with a force of ice pellets, which stung like wasps.

We made it to the house. Dad's hands were shaking as he fumbled through his keys trying to find the one that opened the lock. I blinked, and the tornado was gone. I blinked again, and the rain and wind stopped. I could see that familiar wagon racing toward us from the distance. Fire shot out of the horses nostrils. The clowns were perched high in their seats. Their sinister laughter reverberated through the air, and that annoying jingle-bell sound would not let up. "Hurry, Dad, hurry!" I shouted.

The reins choked the horses' necks "Neigh neigh neigh, they protested. The wagon screeched to a halt. A stone flew out from underneath a wheel, and cracked the front window of our house. "Dad, they brought fire-breathing horses. You got to see this. This is unbelievable!"

"Stop distracting me," he snapped, fumbling with the keys.

I wouldn't take no for an answer. I pulled on his arm until he looked. Dad's eyes seemed like they were about to pop out of his head as he watched two horses puke fire onto our lawn. The flames raced to the mailbox, which went up like a tinderbox. Dad continued tinkering with the lock. "There's something wrong with this. It's jammed. Where's your mother? How come she doesn't open the door to help us?" he asked franticly.

"You forgot to knock. How is she supposed to know we are here?"

Dad started pounding on the door. "Lynn, Lynn, let us in!"

One by one the clowns floated off the wagon toward the ground. Patches carried the pumpkin cane. The eyes of the jack-o'-lantern were on fire. I wondered how he got Noel's pumpkin cane. I could see her giving it to him, or maybe they killed her for it. The three clowns stepped onto the burning grass. They walked through the fire as if it wasn't there. They seemed excited to see Dad and me. They happily waved to us then began to dance around. They did cartwheels and somersaults. Their polka dot clown shirts and striped pants were ripped, and the storm had completely washed away their makeup, unmasking their true faces.

I couldn't believe how much they looked like Lucille. Their faces were living skeletons, just like hers. The only difference—their eyes burned with raging flames. I imagined Lucille lying in the street with flames in her eyes. It was just like the sheriff described it.

Patches waved the pumpkin cane at the horses. They stopped breathing fire, though several small fires continued to burn on our lawn. "Hello, Johnny and Daddy," Aloysius greeted us with a sneer. He removed both fiery eyes from his sockets. He wound up his right arm like a baseball pitcher and threw each of them at us one at a time.

"Watch out!" I shouted as we jumped out of the way. The eyeballs smashed against the door, which began to burn with blue and yellow flames.

"He he he," he snickered.

"What are we going to do now?" I asked.

"This is nuts," Dad answered.

Aloysius appeared to be very happy. "Do you really think I would let you keep my eyes? Return! Return! *Sinda!"*

Dad and I exchanged confused glances. Suddenly, the burning eyeballs flew back out of the door and onto Aloysius's face. He almost fell over from the force of them plowing into his eye sockets. It was magic. Then the door stopped burning. I touched it with my own hand. It was cold.

Sebastian revealed to us a jagged dagger. He waved the blade through the air. "Let's get this over with. I want to cut off their heads."

Patches looked from Sebastian to Aloysius. "Would you and your brother stop screwing around?" he implored.

Sebastian smiled devilishly. "Hey, Johnny, look at this." He hurled his dagger at me. I tried to duck, but the weapon seemed to travel at the speed of light. I felt a tug on my wizard robe. I was stuck to the door by the blade! Luckily, the knife did not cut me.

Dad gave up on the lock and instead focused on trying to free me. Sebastian laughed and jumped up and down. "Hey, Roden, what's it like being an adult?"

"Sebastian, I'm not talking to you."

"Enough of these stupid games!" Patches stepped onto the bottom step of the porch. "Roden, answer the question. You got to grow up. We didn't. What's it like?"

The dagger fell onto the porch. I picked it up and held it in front of me. "You better not come up here!" I warned.

Patches stared evilly at me.

Dad winked at me. "I'm proud of you, son. Thanks for protecting us. Patches, I told you before. I'm not talking to you." Dad returned to the lock.

Patches took another step forward. "What's the rush, Roden? I've missed you. We all have. I want to tell Johnny a story."

Dad threw his hands into the air. "Argh! Damn this cursed lock!"

"Johnny, you are going to like this story," Patches taunted.

I shook the blade at him. "Don't make me stab you!" I nudged Dad and whispered, "Would you hurry up?"

Patches flashed his pointed teeth. "I was sleeping in my cold grave for many years. Then one day I saw a bright light. I followed the light, which led me to my mother. She told me to wake my brothers up, so I did. We followed her into the depths of Hell, where she taught us the blackest magic. Once we learned, we were released. We rode the storm out of Hell and returned to Earth."

"Stop telling lies, Patches!" Dad yelled.

"We found your mom on the street right before she died," I said.

Patches put his head down in sadness. "Yes, we lost her during the storm."

"Why are you trying to kill us?" I asked.

"The price was high to come back. We had to swear revenge on the people who killed us."

"I didn't kill you."

"I know, but your Dad did."

"You did it to yourself, Patches!" Dad raged. "You and your crazy brothers!"

"I thought you weren't talking to us. Yet you keep on talking." Patches pointed the glowing pumpkin cane at the wagon. He spun the cane two circles to the left then three to the right, finishing off with two taps to the sky. "Rise, Kennedy, rise!" A body began to float upward from the back of the wagon. It was Sheriff Kennedy. He had been bound and gagged with vines that had pumpkins growing on them. He made muffled sounds and shook like a fish out of water.

"Dad, they've got the sheriff!"

"Not Kennedy!" Dad exclaimed.

Patches placed the cane at his side. Kennedy fell with a loud thud back into the wagon. "Now it's your father's turn. Did you know we were the best of friends with your Dad, Kennedy, and Virginia when we were children?"

"I didn't know that," I said.

"After we destroy this town, we are taking the three of them with us. We dug up Virginia's grave. She's in the back of the wagon keeping Kennedy company."

I watched the flames rise higher and higher from Patches' eyes. "Where are you going to take them?"

"I can't tell you that, but if you want use your imagination." The jack-o'-lantern cane started laughing, its jaws flapping up and down. *Ha ha ha ha ha ha!*

"I won't let any of you hurt my Dad!"

"He will be hurt." Aloysius cackled.

"What's so funny?" I asked.

"Your love for your father. It won't save him.

I stood my ground. "Shut up!"

Aloysius continued, "Why don't you ask your Daddy about the carnival?"

I looked over at Dad with tears in my eyes. I kept thinking he had lied to me. "You said you didn't kill them."

"Johnny, don't listen to them. What would Lech do when faced with a grave situation like this?"

"That's easy. He would cast a tunnel spell. Send them back to Hell." I pointed my wand at the boys. I had seen every episode of Demon Land, so I knew the passage by heart. I twisted the wand in a clockwise direction, spinning it faster and faster. "Last years, last months, last weeks, last days, last hours, last minutes, last seconds … tunnel!" Nothing happened. "So much for being the great wizard Lech," I sighed.

"You're no wizard, boy!" Aloysius taunted. "Do not pretend to be one."

"You're right." I stripped off my Lech costume and threw it onto the lawn.

Sebastian was rolling around on the ground. He stood on his head. "Johnny, can you do this?"

I ignored him. "Dad, we might die. Did you hear what they said?"

"All I heard was–monsters coming to get us. I won't let them. Superheroes always win against evil!"

"We're not superheroes."

"You're wrong, son. We are. We have to get inside. I need my gun."

"What is that rotten smell?" I asked.

Patches grinned. "It's us. We are living dead kids."

I couldn't get over his missing fingers. I remembered fat Marco inquiring, "Why are they all missing fingers?" They masked themselves so well with magic.

With no warning, a maggot popped out of Patches' arm. He threw it at me. I ducked. It missed hitting me but stuck to the window instead. As I watched it slide down the glass, I wondered if Dad and I had already found hell.

"Finally!" my father shouted. The door opened. We ran inside. Dad bolted the double locks and turned the knob to make sure the door was extra secure. The house was dark. We must have lost power. I could see only a dim light radiating from the kitchen. "Johnny, help me with the hutch." We pushed it up against the front door. "Lynn, Lynn ... where are you?"

The pocket-style kitchen door swung open. Mom came out holding a candle. Her hair was tied back in a ponytail. Her makeup dripped down her face. She was sniffling. She gazed at my father with languished eyes then ran into his arms.

Our house was in shambles. Every picture had fallen off the walls, and the television was smashed. Mom whispered to my father, "What's happening? Who's outside?"

A really loud shrieking voice echoed through the air. "Roden Black, Roden Black ... we are waiting ... remember ... the carnival?"

I pointed at Dad. "Now you are going to tell us the truth! You did something terrible at the carnival. Did you kill those boys?"

"I told you before. Kennedy and I did not kill those kids. Stop doubting me." Mom got in Dad's face. "Did you?"

"No! Would both of you stop? I will take care of this." He turned toward mom. "I love you dear, I always have." He kissed her on the cheek. "Johnny. I love you too ... very much." We smashed fists. He ran upstairs.

"Johnny, who's outside?" Mom asked.

"I don't mean to scare you, but there are living dead kids and fire-breathing horses outside." She fainted. Fortunately, I caught her on the way down, breaking her fall.

Dad returned with a rifle over his shoulder. He dumped a box of shells on the kitchen counter. Some of the bullets rolled onto the floor. "What happened to your mother?" he asked, loading the gun. "Why is she on the floor?"

"I told her the truth about what's going on. She passed out."

"Johnny, how could you? Help me put her on the couch." After we moved mom, Dad broke the front window with the butt of his rifle. The glass spilled onto the porch.

"*Hmm* ... what's this?" *My Halloween candy sack is next to the table. I thought I dropped it when Dad scooped me up to run to the house.* "Dad, I found my treats. You hungry?"

"Johnny, I have a gun out the window right now."

"Well, I'm starving." I dug around through the treats. "Ooh, who gave me this? A chocolate pumpkin with glowing orange candy sparkles. I wondered how the candy glowed.

Dad had his finger on the trigger, but he didn't squeeze. He paused to comment. "I use to eat those when I was a kid. I haven't seen that candy in twenty years."

I popped the pumpkin into my mouth. "*Mmm* ... so tasty. It's delicious."

I looked at my hands. They were slowly disappearing. The air was eating me! In a matter of seconds, my entire body became completely invisible!

"Johnny!" Dad shouted in a panic. He tried to grab me but fell through me like I wasn't there. "Come back, Johnny, come back!"

I thought I only turned invisible, but Dad's voice faded away as if I also left the house. I tried to open my eyes, pushing and pushing my eyelids. Nothing happened. It was like they had been sealed shut. I couldn't see anything except colored lights flickering off the back of my eyeballs. I could sense these lights taking me somewhere far away. Was I flying? It felt like I was. At last the chocolate taste slipped away.

Chapter 10
The Haunted Carnival

I could hear a dog barking in the distance. I opened my eyes and found myself lying in a pile of fallen tree leaves looking up at the setting sun. I felt around my face. I touched my arms, my stomach, and my hands. Where was I? Did I take a time warp somewhere? Was I still in Whisper?

The house, Dad, Mom, and the living dead kids were gone. The barking dog got closer and closer. My eyes met the sad eyes of a black and tan German Shepherd. He continued to bark. "Do you know where I am, boy?" I asked. Of course, he did not answer. I was surprised he held his bark; instead, he licked my face and let me pet him. "Okay, okay." I hugged the dog and took a friendly roll in the leaves with him.

I was happy to be away from all that evil. *Wait a minute. What about Mom and Dad?* I could see Dad shooting out the window at the living dead kids and my mom still passed out on the couch.

Brushing the leaves off, I addressed the dog: "I have to find the way home. Can you help?" The dog's pointy ears turned up. He tilted his head while giving me a funny look. He started barking again then ran away toward a winding trail. I ran after him into the shadowy woods. Suddenly, I heard people talking and laughing.

I entered a clearing marked by a black metal gate with a sign on it that read "Haunted Halloween Carnival" in white flashing lights. I hung my arms over the top of the gate to get a better look. Hordes of people walked around. Most of the kids were dressed in Halloween costumes. I saw spooky carnival rides, games, and a giant Ferris wheel decorated with bright colored lights. *I think that's the one Jimmy and Jay talked about.* Did my Halloween candy teleport me into Whisper's past?

I pushed the gate open and walked through. Someone tapped me on the shoulder. "Hey, kid. Where do you think you are going?" A scary-looking man towered over me. He was about seven feet tall and wore a devil's mask and a long black coat with a matching top hat. Red, triangle-shaped wings extended from the back of his coat high into the air. They flapped up and down as he spoke in a demonic voice: "I can't let you in without a carnival ticket."

"Ticket, what?" I stumbled over my words. "I don't—"

"Relax, kid. I know I'm scary, but you gotta have a ticket to get in. Why don't you check your pockets? I'm sure mommy or Daddy must have bought you one." I dug through my pockets. "Come on. I haven't got all day." The devil man grinned showing silvery teeth that looked like fangs. "Want to see my tongue? Most people have to pay, but for you today is free."

"All right," I said hesitantly.

He stuck his tongue out, slithering it like a snake. It was very long and split into three sections. One slithered to the right, another to the left, and the last dangled in the middle. My eyes almost crossed as his tongue missed reaching my nose by only an inch. He was a monster. "They call me the Three-Tongued Devil. What do you think of my tongues?"

I wondered if he was the real devil from Hell. I felt very afraid. I had trouble getting my words out. "Uh ... I don't ... are you going to eat me now?"

The devil man roared with laughter. "No, kid."

I sighed in relief. "Well, I feel better. I found the ticket." I held it up. "Admit One, Haunted Halloween Carnival," it read.

"No one likes my tongues. I like to terrify people. Later I'm starring in a haunted house show. Come check it out. I'll make you pee your pants."

"Sounds like fun. I love peeing my pants."

"You're funny, kid." The devil man took off his hat and held it out. "Drop the ticket in then you are free to wander the carnival."

I couldn't get over the big horns on his head hiding under his top hat. I let go of the ticket. It floated into the upturned hat like a feather in slow motion. Then a flash, like someone taking a picture, followed by a puff of smoke. The hat and devil man had disappeared. I swear I saw wings in the sky.

Not sure what just happened, I made my way into the crowded carnival. I stopped in front of a carousel to watch children and winged ponies go in circles. It looked like any second now they would take flight. I watched a kid dressed as a mummy. He laughed hysterically while holding onto the gold spiral pole coming out of a pony's back. His father, sitting on the pony in front of him, made funny faces. The scene made me think of my dad.

A game called "Hang the Skeleton" caught my attention. Two kids played side by side: a boy dressed as a monk and a girl in a painter costume with brushes peaking out of her blotched smock. Each child stood in a chalk-outlined box. The object of the game was to throw a noose over a skeleton's head. It cost a quarter to get three shots. The girl hung her skeleton on her last throw. She chose a giant stuffed monkey as her prize.

I got in a line of at least ten people for "Monster Candy Balloons." I never had a monster candy balloon or even heard of one. The coolest costume I saw in line was worn by the lady in front of me. She was dressed as a gypsy with long white hair stuffed under a moon-and star-covered bandana, a purple velvet shawl featuring matching moons and stars, and giant silver hoop earrings dangling from her ears. Her arms were covered with shiny bracelets; her neck, beaded jewelry. She carried a thick black book called Magic: The Art of Rising. I tapped her on the shoulder. "Excuse me ma'am. What is that book you are reading?"

She smiled. "It's a spell book. Did you ever cast a magic spell at the stroke of midnight?"

I shook my head. "Will you show me?"

She opened the book to let me skim over a few pages. I saw step-by-step diagrams of how to cast spells. One was called, "How to raise the dead." I immediately took a long hard look at the lady. Her eyes were black as the night. I couldn't believe it. The lady was Lucille. I glimpsed a flash of her dying again in the road.

I grabbed the book and struggled with her to take it out of her hands. I wanted to know more about the raise-the-dead spell. I had a very strong feeling she used this spell to raise her own sons from the dead. But she wouldn't release the book. "No! You saw enough!" she shouted, shutting the book and shoving it in her satchel. She turned away from me to get her monster candy balloon. "Thanks sis," she said to the woman working the counter.

"Come over tomorrow for dinner. I will make my famous piggy chops," the woman responded, handing her a balloon.

"Sounds great. I'll bring the boys." Lucille walked past me with her high-flying balloon. It looked like a ghost.

"Ok, sonny, how many?" the balloon woman asked.

I placed my elbows on the counter. "One monster balloon, please."

The woman looked familiar with her granny glasses, caked-on-makeup face, and blond wig. "That will be twenty-five cents," she said.

"Is your name Noel?" I asked.

She looked confused. "How do you know my name?"

"Your sister said it before she walked away."

"*Huh.* I don't remember that." She took a sip of tea.

"I have another question. What is a monster candy balloon?"

"It's a monster-shaped balloon with a piece of candy hidden inside."

"Do I get to pick the monster?"

"No. It's random. Most people enjoy the balloon until the helium runs low then they pop it and eat the candy."

"I like when balloons pop."

"Oh yes. Some people pop them right after they buy them. We have to speed this up. I have a lot of people waiting behind you."

I turned out my pockets. I didn't even have a penny. "I'm sorry. I made a mistake. I have no money."

She shook her head. She seemed mad at me. I left empty-handed.

I found a weeping willow to sit under and collect my thoughts. *Maybe I'm here to stop Lucille from raising her sons from the dead. I wish I got that spell book from her. I can't believe her sister Noel is here. I wonder who else is.* I could hear balloons popping all around me.

"You can get brain damage doing that," said a voice above me. Two hands pulled me up from my sitting position on the ground.

"Doing what?" I asked.

"Thinking. Where have you been? I've been looking all over for you." A kid around my age jumped out of the tree and stood in front of me. He was dressed as a baseball player in a striped uniform, ball cap and glove. Number eleven was on his shirt.

"Who are you?" I asked.

"I guess you did get brain damage. Very funny, Roden."

Roden? That's Dad's name. I had returned to my father's past as him. "Kennedy," I guessed.

"Yeah. Come on. We are running late. The Bipimtaff brothers told me to meet them at the jack-o'-lantern contest."

"Sounds great. I'm quite the pumpkin critic."

"I know. You tell me every year. Great titanium death glasses, Roden. I know you said you don't, but you do look like the monster doctor from that show *Killing the Ghosts*. What happened to your axe? You had it an hour ago."

"I don't know. I guess I lost it." I smiled at myself. Dad once upon a time did dress up for Halloween. I followed Kennedy to a haunted house, which was an old red barn. "Why are we going to the haunted house? I thought you said the pumpkin contest."

"I messed up. I kept thinking about coming to the haunted house, so here we are."

"That's all right, Kennedy. Haunted houses are fun."

The barn's windows were all boarded up. Bales of hay had been arranged to create a walkway leading to the front gate. The devil man sat on a bale next to the gate. Scary music played over loudspeakers. "Doom music," I observed.

The devil man evilly laughed at us. "Welcome to my haunted house. Get ready to be scared!"

Kennedy rolled up his sleeves. "I love being scared, and I like your music."

"Thanks, kid. It's funeral music. No one makes it out of my haunted house alive." I could hear people inside the barn screaming and pounding on the walls.

"Should we go in?" I asked Kennedy.

He looked at his wristwatch. "Damn, it's ten of eight. My plan was to go in, but we have to meet the Bibimtaff brothers in a few minutes. They've got something big planned for tonight."

"What do they have planned?"

"You will have to wait and see," Kennedy teased.

I had a bad feeling in my stomach about meeting them. The devil man was nowhere to be found. Maybe there wasn't enough screaming in the haunted house, so he went inside.

Chapter 11
The Jack-o 'Lantern Contest

Kennedy waved to me. "Let's go. The jack-o 'lantern contest awaits. We don't want to miss it."

I saw something that made me stop in my tracks. It was the farm wagon with the ARNIVAL sign. I remembered the living dead kids riding to town in it. Two black horses were harnessed to the front of the wagon. The back was full of pumpkins. A man was sitting next to it in a wooden chair marked with a big sign that read: "Pumpkins 10 cents each." He was wearing overalls and a floppy hat, which was pulled down over his eyes. The way his legs were crossed made me think he was sleeping. "Is that—" I shouted at him. "Mr. Johnson! Mr. Johnson!"

Kennedy nudged me. "What are you doing? Let him sleep. Like I said before, we got something big planned for tonight. We don't want to mess it up." Was I about to relive what Dad had been hiding all these years? "See you later, Mr. Johnson," Kennedy whispered.

We finally arrived at the jack-o'-lantern contest. I was happy to see lots of children and adults sitting on bales of hay waiting for the show to begin.

"Must be 100 people here," I commented.

Kennedy took off his baseball glove. "It's popular."

Most of the people were eating candy and drinking pop. Everyone was talking about his or her pumpkin and how they were going to win. The stage was lit up with glowing torches on all sides except in the front where a long wooden table stood. It had a row of unlit jack-o'-lanterns on it. I counted twenty. A microphone and stand was set up to the side.

A man carrying a cane emerged from the shadows behind the stage. He was dressed in a flashy purple suit with tin buttons running down the front. A jack-o'-lantern mask covered his face. He grabbed the microphone. "For those of you who don't know me, my name is Almon. For those of you who do know me, welcome back." Tap. Tap. Tap. Almon struck the end of his cane against the stage. Everyone quieted down.

"Looks like it's going to be a good show. Let's check it out," Kennedy suggested.

I scanned the rows. "Where do we sit? All the seats are full."

A girl around our age with a very pretty voice called out to us. "Over hear. I saved you some seats." I followed Kennedy. We sat down on a bale next to her. She kept smiling and making eyes at me. "Hi, Roden," she said. "Want a gumdrop?"

At first the way she was looking at me caused me to feel uneasy, but she was really cute. I smiled as she handed me the gumdrop. "Who's that?" I whispered to Kennedy.

"Are you serious? It's Virginia. She's only had a crush on you since first grade. You are acting so weird today."

She wore a yellow-jacket costume with wings, and her hair was done up like a beehive.

It reminded me of Sister Virginia. Come to think of it, I was sure she was a young Sister Virginia. I couldn't believe a nun used to have a crush on my Dad! "Thanks, Sister Virginia."

"Did you just refer to me as a nun?" she asked.

"You heard me wrong. Sweet Virginia," I corrected myself.

She giggled. "I like that."

We started watching the show. "Welcome to the annual Halloween jack-o'-lantern contest. I know all of you worked hard on bringing your best pumpkin to life," said Almon. One by one he lit the jack-o'-lanterns. Within minutes the table looked like it was on fire with glowing spooktacular jack-o'-lanterns. He held his cane high into the air. The jack-o'-lantern face on the cane lit up. He shouted, "This cane is the prize for best of the year!"

Everyone shouted and clapped. "I can't believe he's got the magic pumpkin cane," I said to Virginia.

"He didn't say it was a magic cane."

"It is, Virginia. I have to get my hands on that cane."

Virginia got the giggles again. "If the cane is made of magic, do you think you could make Kennedy disappear?"

Kennedy and I laughed. "You can't win the cane if you didn't carve a pumpkin," he explained.

"I did," Virginia said. "Mine is the smiley-face one."

"Why did you carve a happy pumpkin?" Kennedy asked.

"Halloween is happy," she replied.

"No." He curled his hands like monster claws. "It's spooky and scary. It's supposed to have hellion eyes and killer teeth."

Almon addressed the crowd again. "As you all know, I am a storyteller. I have a great story this year, so listen up. Be scared." He sat down in the middle of the stage with his black boots hanging over the edge. He laid the pumpkin cane across his lap. I looked around at all the people watching. They couldn't wait for him to begin.

"I was in Salem last month studying the 1692 witch trials. I have always been fascinated by witches. I encountered a real witch on my journey. I went home with her to her castle. As I wandered the castle corridors, I became mystified by the bizarre artwork on the walls. This is what I saw: pictures of demons holding up worlds, a spell-casting session in a cemetery, a horned beast savagely eating the moon, and three burning witches hanging from a tree."

"She took me into her room of sorcery where she conjured spells. The room contained books, scrolls, potions, and a collection of scepters. This cane caught my eye." He held the pumpkin cane in the air. "I asked her if I could have it. She surprised me when she gave it to me. She told me that the cane once belonged to the lord of the jack-o'-lanterns, and it was made of magic."

"Told you so," I said.

"The jack-o'-lantern lord was worshiped—
"

"Your story sucks!" someone interrupted. "Get off the stage!"

"It's a lie!" Someone else called out. "Nobody wants to hear about a jack-o'-lantern lord, pumpkins, or witches."

Kennedy smirked. "The Bipimtaff brothers are here." He waved to them as they walked toward us wearing their evil-clown costumes.

I was mad. "They're messing everything up!"

"It's a stupid story, Roden. So fake," Kennedy complained.

"Sorry, Roden. I like you, but I have to agree with Kennedy," Virginia offered.

I ignored them and spoke my mind. "Almon, tell us more!"

A man in the audience scolded the menacing Bipimtaff brothers. "You kids, shut up and get out of here!"

Patches yelled back: "you better watch it. We'll kick your ass!"

The man stood up in defiance. He towered over the brothers. He was dressed like a hillbilly with a goofy cowboy hat and bucked teeth. "I'll fight you punks, right now!"

Seeing the full size of the man, Patches seemed discouraged. "Another time. We are out of here."

"That's what I thought." The hillbilly sat back down.

Patches pointed at Kennedy as he walked by. "It's time," he said. The brothers walked behind the stage. The crowd booed them as they left.

Almon resumed speaking from the stage. "Let's give Lex, the hillbilly, a round of applause for getting rid of those hooligans." Everyone clapped.

"All right, Halloween fans. Let's get to what we came here for. Time to vote. Everyone come up to cast your ballot in the box next to the jack-o'-lantern you like best." He displayed the pumpkin cane again. "Remember, best jack-o'-lantern wins the pumpkin cane."

Row by row the people started to vote. Almon prepared to leave the stage. *What? That's it? I have unanswered questions.* I asked as loudly as I could, "Almon, what about the rest of the story?" He ignored my query. My chance to find out more about the pumpkin cane was blown. It once belonged to the lord of the jack-o'-lanterns that I did learn.

"Come on, Roden, they're waiting on us," Kennedy said.

"What about the contest?"

"What about it? We've got to discuss the plan."

"All right," I said.

"Where are you guys going?" Virginia asked.

"Don't worry about it. You should stay to see if your corny jack-o'-lantern wins," Kennedy answered.

"You are a jerk! If Roden is going with you then I'm going too," Virginia insisted.

"Could be dangerous," I explained.

"If I go, Roden, will you be my hero and protect me?"

"I will do my best," I answered. She smiled and kissed me on the lips. I blushed.

Kennedy broke up our moment. "Come on, let's go, lovebirds." The three us left the jack-o'-lantern contest to go behind the stage. The Bipimtaff brothers were huddled in a small circle. They saw us and let us in. Kennedy slapped each one of their hands. Aloysius was smoking a cigarette and blowing rings.

"Hey," I greeted them. "Nice clown costumes."

All three nodded at me. "You shouldn't smoke," Virginia said.

"Who's this girl?" asked Aloysius.

"A friend," Kennedy answered. "We could use her as a diversion."

"Why are all of you dressed as clowns?" she asked.

"Bipimtaff brothers always dress the same. It's Halloween tradition. Our costumes are better than yours, Beehead," Patches boasted. Everyone started laughing. The name-calling definitely broke up the tension. "Listen up, Beebreath. What we are about to do is more wicked than a blizzard on a summer day. Why would we want you helping us?" He grabbed a handful of her beehive hair. "Wow, this is thick!" he exclaimed.

I pulled his hand away from her. "Leave her alone!"

She looked at me with that school-girl crush again. "I'll be your diversion. Just tell me what to do," she pleaded.

"Patches, what do you have planned?" I asked.

"Steal Mr. Johnson's pumpkin wagon and take it for a wild ride up and down Rattlesnake Mountain."

"Have you ever driven a horse-drawn wagon?" I inquired skeptically.

Patches straightened his jingly joker hat. "None of us have. It's going to be a devil's moon tonight."

"Where does Virginia fit in?" I asked.

She pointed to Rattlesnake Mountain not far from where we were standing. "You guys are crazy. If you go up there, you are going to die! The trail on the mountain is way too narrow. Let's go back to the carnival. Forget about this."

No one responded. We just stood there dreaming about the mountain. Under the full moon, its peaks and treetops shone like a painted landscape.

Finally, Patches spoke up. "I can't wait to ride that pass. Feel the wind in my hair. I'm going to say this once. Any wimps who don't want to go down in history with me can leave now. Everyone looked at one another. No one moved. Not even Virginia. "Beehead, all you have to do is distract Mr. Johnson long enough for us to steal his wagon," he explained.

Virginia was playing with her lip. "How?"

"That's easy. Talk to him about his alien fruits and vegetables," I said.

"Great idea, Roden."

"I have a rock in my shoe." Sebastian took off his left giant clown shoe to dig around for it. Virginia looked at the ground. "May God forgive me. I'll do it."

"Good," Patches said. "When we steal the wagon, anyone dressed like a clown gets to sit in front; anyone who's not, in the back."

"Hey, wait a minute. I want to ride in front," Kennedy demanded.

"Next crime. This is *our* show," Patches declared.

"You're right," Kennedy agreed. "It was your plan. Let's just do this."

The six of us armed ourselves with our toughest faces. We were on our way to find Mr. Johnson and his wagon full of pumpkins.

Chapter 12
Natures Beast

My new friends and I were like hungry cats in search of prey. We blended in with the nighttime carnival while keeping to ourselves. Mr. Johnson was our prey. We walked two by two: Patches in front with Sebastian, Virginia and Aloysius next and Kennedy and me in the back. "So, you ready to be a legend?" Kennedy asked.

I rolled my eyes. I couldn't help it. "I guess."

He could tell I felt uneasy. He slapped me on the back. "Don't worry. This is gonna be fun."

"You really like this, don't you?"

"This is the best," he answered.

"You okay up there Virginia?" I asked.

She turned around to look at me. "I'm good," She said nervously.

My stomach was in knots. I knew I had to relive what Dad lived, but I was afraid. I probably put Virginia in jeopardy. I bet Dad put her in jeopardy, too. I wondered what Dad would do in the future. Would he finally stop the living dead kids? If so, then why was I still here? What about Lucille and her sister Noel? Would I see them again before I most likely would die? How about my mom? Was she okay? I bet my brothers Jimmy and Jay were still trick or treating, even if Whisper was in the midst of chaos. *I wanted to go home.*

We ducked behind the apple cider stand. The aroma of apples and cinnamon made me crave some cider. Everyone kept peeking around the corner to see what Mr. Johnson was doing. We watched him sell a pumpkin to a couple dressed as bandits. Even though we looked sneaky lurking around the stand, no one paid us any attention-not even the girl selling cider.

"Everyone ready?" Patches whispered.

We all nodded. "All right, Beehead, you're on."

Virginia reached out in a friendly way toward Patches. He must have thought she wanted to shake his hand. Instead she pinched the top of it as hard as she could until he let out a squeamish cry. With a twist of her hip, she walked away to do her thing. Everyone laughed except Patches.

"You keep calling her Beehead. It's not right," I told him in a quiet voice.

He grabbed me and shook me violently. "Mind your own business, Roden!"

"Relax, you are on the edge. Stop shaking me!"

"You know what? You're right." He let go of me. "Sorry, I lost it for a minute there."

"It's all right. I can understand you being crazy for what's about to go down." But I did wonder what was up with Patches and Virginia. *Why was he so mean to her?*

She approached Mr. Johnson as he sat in his chair. She ruffled her wings and made bee sounds. "Hello, young lady. What a cute costume," he commented in that slow tired voice I remembered.

At first her words were shaky. "Tha—thank you. How are you?"

"I'm good. Aren't carnivals exciting?"

"They are. Mr. Johnson, can I ask you something?"

"Of course."

"I'm curious about your alien plants. Would you tell me about them?

He chuckled. "How did you know about my aliens?"

"Everybody knows."

He laughed again. "I suppose so." He pointed up. "I saw a flying saucer one night in the sky many years ago. The very next day I found a 600-pound pumpkin in my patch."

Virginia leaned toward him to listen as hard as she could. "That's amazing. I've never seen a pumpkin that big. Tell me more."

"I thought I was just having a God's gift grow that year, but that was not the case. Around the same time the following year, I found a complete harvest of five-pound, star-shaped peanuts. The next year came with giant carrots that looked like snowflakes. It was always something different every year."

"Carrots, snowflakes. Santa would love those! What did they leave behind this year?"

"Nothing. I'm still waiting."

"What do the aliens look like?" Virginia looked in our direction and waved us forward.

Mr. Johnson scratched his head. "You know, I'm not sure. I never saw their faces—just their ship. Who you waving at?"

"I wasn't waving. I was trying to swoosh a fly away. What does their spaceship look like?"

"Kind of like a glowing life vest." Virginia giggled.

I was glad to see that Mr. Johnson hadn't changed from all those years ago. His alien story was his grand prize. I wondered what it would be like to carve a 600-pound pumpkin. After I turned it into a jack-o'-lantern, I could live in it.

The five of us moved swiftly. We approached from behind. That way Mr. Johnson couldn't see us coming. His horses, however, looked at us with giant eyes and long faces. The Bipimtaff brothers got in the front of the wagon. Kennedy and I slipped into the back with all the pumpkins. The wagon shook.

"What was that noise?" Mr. Johnson asked.

"I didn't hear anything," Virginia replied.

Patches slammed the reins into the horses' backs. "Move beasts! Move!" he shouted. *Neigh neigh neigh.* The horses bucked up and down. Then like a fast car the wagon took off. Patches would not let up for a second in beating the horses with the reins.

Mr. Johnson started running toward the wagon. "Stop! What are you doing? Come back!" Unbelievably, he caught up to us like in an old western movie. He grabbed the back of the wagon and tried to climb in. But Kennedy pounded on his hands with his fists until Mr. Johnson let go. He tumbled a few feet onto the ground. He came up with a mouthful of grass. I felt awful for him. I liked Mr. Johnson a lot. "Stop that wagon!" he yelled.

A few people came to his rescue. They shouted and chased after us. No way could they catch us, though. We were too fast and too far away, by this point. "I know a short cut to the mountain," Patches said to his brothers.

The wagon bounced and shook, causing the pumpkins to roll around on top of us. I could still see Virginia, so I gave her a goodbye wave. She waved back. I knew I most likely wouldn't see her ever again. This was a very bad idea that was already getting her in trouble. I could tell, Mr. Johnson was yelling at her because his lips were moving too fast to be speaking normally. I couldn't hear his words, but I felt them with all the finger-pointing and fist-shaking. Moments later both of them faded out of sight.

We arrived at Rattlesnake Mountain. Up we went. Trees and shrubs flew by. The full moon looked unreal. It was so large. The rumbling sounds of the horses' heavy hooves shook the ground below us. Rocks and dirt rolled down the mountainside. Kennedy stood up, unsteadily. "Yeah! We're going to be legends!" he screamed like a maniac. The Bibimtaff brothers each raised a hand behind them. Kennedy slapped all three then continued screaming nonsense. Everyone looked proud.

What was wrong with these kids? How could Dad have friends like these? I shouted to the front of the wagon: "Where are we going, Patches?"

"To the top! We are flying straight to the top," he answered, triumphantly.

Kennedy pointed with his mouth open. "What is *tha*—?"

"Must be 10,000 of them!" I marveled, gazing at the bats overhead. I thought back to what Lucille said about fruit bats digging in her garden. Thousands of them ate all the pumpkin seeds across the land before flying off to the place of departed spirits. It started to rain, but the droplets did not feel like rain. They felt like little pieces of wood. I caught some in my hand and couldn't believe what I saw. They were *pumpkin seeds*. Kennedy had them in his hair. So did the Bipimtaff brothers. "This is a bad sign!" I shouted so everyone would hear.

Aloysius turned around while picking seeds from his hair. "A sign for what?"

"A witch is conjuring a spell somewhere close*." I could see us crashing down the mountain really soon. I was running out of time.*

"Why am I covered in sunflower seeds?" Kennedy asked.

"Not sunflower seeds. Pumpkin seeds," I corrected him.

Kennedy outlined the number eleven on his baseball jersey with his finger. "I have never been in a pumpkin seed storm. This is freaky, like that show The Twilight Zone. Hey, do you guys think I could hit one of those bats with a pumpkin?"

"I want to try that," Sebastian answered back.

"I'm after you," Aloysius said.

Kennedy picked up a pumpkin and hurled it toward the bats. He didn't even come close. I was getting mad. No one paid any attention to what I had said. I had to tell them. Maybe I was here to change the past, which would save the future. "Everyone! Stop talking!" I shouted at the top of my lungs. This got everyone's attention. They all looked at me like I was out of my mind. "Did you guys not hear what I said about the witch?"

Patches had been quiet for far too long. "Who cares? It's Halloween."

"Patches, you've got to listen to me. Don't you think it is strange that thousands of bats are flying above us and raining pumpkin seeds down on top of us?"

"I do, but I'm enjoying the ride right now. Look at that moon and those bats! Wow!"

Kennedy threw another pumpkin at them. He missed again. He tried a third time. Frustrated, I grabbed his arms and pushed them down until he dropped the next pumpkin. He shoved me back. "Hey! What's your problem?"

I pointed at the Bipimtaff brothers one by one. "Your mother is casting a spell right now. We are caught in the middle of it. You guys are going to die. She will bring you back from the dead and turn you into monsters." All three brothers started laughing hysterically.

Kennedy joined in the laughter. "What about me? What happens to me?"

"You live," I answered.

"Why am I the lucky one?"

"I don't know, Kennedy. That's just the way it happens."

Patches took his eyes off the path to flash me a spooky smile. "How about you, Roden? What happens to you?"

I shook my head. "I'm not Roden. My name is Johnny. I'm Roden's son from the future."

Suddenly, I didn't feel the pumpkin seeds hitting my body anymore. I put my hand out. The seed storm was gone. The wagon began to shake violently. I could feel the wheels slipping. The horses' neighs were screams.

Patches yelled, "Look at the sky! Something is happening to the sky!"

The army of bats began flying away from the full moon and toward us. The closer they got, the more the bats shrieked. They swooped down and attacked us with biting and scratching. In a frantic voice, Patches cried: "Oh … *shit*!"

The wagon spun out of control. It flipped off the path. Kennedy yelled, "Jump! Everyone jump!"

I tried to jump, but my legs wouldn't go. It was like I was forced to stay inside the wagon. I watched Kennedy fall into a bush while the Bipimtaff brothers and I crashed down the mountain with the wagon and horses.

Chapter 13
Spell Land

I shut my eyes to welcome my certain death as we continued plummeting down the mountainside. At the same time, I was thinking about how I didn't change a thing. I failed. *Why was I sent to the past anyway?* Seconds went by ... then minutes ... no crash. *Why is it taking so long to reach the ground?* All I could feel was the blackness around me pushing in on me.

This reminded me of the sensation I had when I left Mom and Dad's house to come to this horrible place. I thought about Dad and what he would say or do to get me to open my eyes. Then he appeared in physical form in my head. He was wearing an all-white cloak. Maybe he was an angel. He pulled down his hood and handed me a rifle. "What do you want me to do?" I asked.

"Shoot the living dead kids," he said. Then he disappeared.

A red blob covered the shaft of the rifle. I wasn't sure what it was-maybe blood. The blob slowly oozed down the rifle. I could sense that we were about to hit the ground. At the same time, I became even more lost inside my head. A thick fog blocked my vision. I squinted as hard as I could to see through the fog. I can't see anything. A minute later the fog lifted.

Lucille stood outside a cave with the spellbook that I remembered her having at the carnival. The book was open and floating in the air. She was calling out to a lightning filled dark sky. The high notes she hit could have cracked glass. "Pumpkin rain! Raging bats! Take me into death's storm!" She glared at me with fiery eyes then waved the pumpkin cane at me.

I squeezed the trigger on what was left of the blob-covered rifle. It didn't fire. The rest of the gun melted in my hands. Next I heard a loud *bang, pop and smash*. We had crashed. I couldn't see a thing. *Was I dead? What was that stabbing pain in my legs, arms, hands, and eyes?* I cried out, "*Arrh!* Stop it! It hurts!"

I surprised myself when I opened my eyes to a band of miniature flying demons with bulging fish eyes, steel teeth, and long snaky tails. They were poking me with pitchforks like I was a voodoo doll. I counted ten of these demonic beasts while batting at them with my fists. I punched one. The thing screeched. Its rubbery skin felt squishy, like goo. Wait a minute. I saw this episode of *Demon Land*. It was called "Attack of the Jelly Demons."

What's going on here? Why is everything in slow motion? I'm tumbling in outer space like a baby alien as these stupid demons poke me every few seconds. I cried out again, "I told you before! Leave me alone! Somebody help me!" Suddenly, I stopped tumbling.

Next I found myself walking down a hallway away from the jelly demons. I heard a door slam. The demons disappeared. I entered a bright tunnel. *Was heaven around the bend?* Something pushed me along. I kept looking behind me. No one was there. After walking for a long time, the light inside the tunnel began to fade to black. It was dark again. I wished I had a flashlight.

The song "Moby" popped into my head. I whistled it to keep myself from being afraid. "Is anyone there? If you are … would you please … turn the light on?" I thought back to the moment when Lucille died in the road. Why didn't we leave her there and keep driving?

The tunnel ended with me hitting my face against an invisible wall. I felt around through the blackness. The wall was smooth like stone and the coldest thing I had ever touched. My body began to shiver. Soon I was freezing. My hands went numb. A thick layer of ice formed on them. I clapped them together to break the ice. Something shattered against the floor. "Oh my God! My hands fell off!" I shouted.

I fell to my knees. My arms were also icing over. I'm falling apart, I thought. Why is this happening? I can't take it anymore. I heard the sound of more breaking ice. I couldn't feel my arms. Then they were gone!

I believed my eyes were playing tricks on me because I glimpsed a glimmer of light shining through the wall. The light was zapping on and off like a flashing sign. How could I get to that light? My body was frozen. What was left of me smashed against the floor.

The light came on in the tunnel. Lucille, above me, lit the tunnel with the pumpkin cane.

Though I was only broken pieces of ice lying on the floor, somehow I managed to see her.

One by one she picked up the ice pieces of my body and built herself a giant axe. She used it to smash through the wall with me. We tumbled past the floating stones into outer space toward the light.

Before long a city of fire appeared in front of us. There was the Arnival wagon. Lucille swung the axe, and I cut the chains of the wagon. It took off through the flames into a lighting- filled sky. *I think I just freed the Bibimtaff brothers from Hell.*

Chapter 14
City of Fire

I heard a voice that didn't belong in the city of fire. "Johnny! Wake up! Wake up! Wake up! it shouted. *Was it my dad calling?* I opened my eyes.

"Why are you crying, Dad?" I asked.

He cradled me in his arms. He kissed me on the forehead and gave me a loving hug. He had the biggest smile on his face that I'd ever seen. "Oh my God! Welcome back. After you ate that candy, you passed out. You have been unconscious for hours. A couple of minutes ago your body started shaking, and your eyes were rolling around in your head. I thought you were going to die."

"Lucille turned me into an ice axe. I freed the Bibimtaff brothers from Hell. And I was you ... Dad ... at the Halloween carnival."

Dad's face turned what can only be described as green. "Did you hit your head?

"No, I didn't hit my head."

"That makes me feel better. I was afraid you might have brain damage! Now tell me slowly what happened."

I plopped down into the big-armed purple chair. The cushion sunk, and I took a few deep breaths to help me relax. I watched the ticking hand on the sun-shaped wall clock. "Dad, I saw the whole thing. How you, Kennedy, and the Bibimtaff brothers stole Mr. Johnson's wagon. I rode that wagon up Rattlesnake Mountain with your crazy friends. When it came time to jump off the wagon, I didn't. I couldn't. Unknown forces made me stay inside. I'm almost positive it was Lucille and one of her spells that kept me in there. We crashed down the mountain."

"The Bibimtaff brothers died. I thought I was dead too, but I could still see things. I started seeing visions of demons and being lost. My body froze and fell apart. Lucille built an axe made of ice out of my frozen body parts. She used me to smash through a wall then we flew into Hell."

"Lucille hovered over a flowing river of fire with me in her right hand. She was waiting for something. I watched her eyes search the flames like a hawk. Smoky gray and black shapes of people and beasts tried to escape the fire. All attempts were unsuccessful, however, as the fire sucked them back down, and the river pushed them along. I heard cries of pain and blood-curdling screams. I wasn't sure where any person or beast was going. There was no way out of the fire because it was everywhere."

"Some time passed. Then it happened. I couldn't believe it when I saw the wagon ride by. It was chained to blue and yellow flames, and the Bipimtaff brothers were sitting up front. Stretching the wagon's chains, the horses kept trying to pull it out of the fire. Lucille waved to her burning children. 'Don't worry. Mommy is coming, boys!' She dove into the fire and cut the chains using me as her axe. Then she left me to melt in the inferno. I watched her and her boys ride out of the city of fire. Their wagon disappeared into a bolt of lightning. After that I only remember opening my eyes and seeing your smiling face."

Dad looked mesmerized. "Holy shit! I think you went to Hell. Did you see the devil?"

"No, but I did see a winged devil man at the Halloween carnival. He was like seven feet tall. He was the one who let me into the carnival. Kennedy and I almost went into his haunted house, but we didn't because we were late for a meeting with the Bibimtaff brothers."

Dad grabbed the box of bullets off the table. He looked inside then shook his head. "Not good. We don't have a lot of shots left. We are going to need more firepower."

"That's all you're going to say about what happened?"

"You know ... I've had a rough night, too. Would you let me think for a minute?"

"Okay." I went to get a glass of water.

"Johnny, I would bet anything that the guy you saw was the devil himself because there was no devil man at any Halloween carnival when I was a kid," he explained when I returned. "One thing I don't get is that if Lucille set her sons free from Hell then how did they get there? They didn't kill anyone but themselves. It doesn't make sense."

"You are right. It makes no sense. Dad, I couldn't believe the stuff I saw. I liked how Sister Virginia had a crush on you!"

"Yeah, I remember that. It was sweet until I corrupted her. Who knows? Maybe because of that night she became a nun."

"I liked her. There is another thing I found out that makes me happy."

"What's that?"

"You didn't kill the Bipimtaff brothers."

"I told you before. I'm not a killer."

I looked around the room. My mom was still passed out on the couch, and the floor was riddled with bullet shells.

"Did you stop the living dead kids?" Dad asked. One of the front windows shattered. A pumpkin rolled toward me. I kicked it to the side of the room. "I guess that answers my question. Johnny, we are still at war. I need you to be a soldier. I need to get back to shooting. Will you wake your mom up and take her upstairs? It's safe up there for now. Put her in my bedroom. Then come back."

"All right."

Dad returned to his rifle, which lay against the window sill. He picked up the weapon, loaded it, and pointed it out the window. "Feel my rage!" he shouted as he shot a round into the night. He sounded like a psycho. He was really getting into this.

"Mom, wake up!" I urged.

"Johnny, what happened?"

"You fainted. I need to help you upstairs. Don't worry. Dad and I got this." I was surprised that she did not question what Dad and I were doing. But she did have a frightened look in her eyes as I steered her. I tucked her into bed and gave her a kiss on the cheek.

"You ever fire a gun?" Dad inquired, when I went back downstairs.

"No. You know that. But I always wanted to."

"Now is your chance." He handed me his rifle. It was just as I dreamed. "All you have to do is aim and squeeze the trigger."

"You need a gun."

"Hold on." He opened the coat closet next to the fireplace and came back with a shotgun. "See? I told you we needed more firepower."

"Where did you get that?"

"Thirtieth Birthday present from Uncle Lex. You ready to do this?"

I put my fist out, and Dad smashed it.

Chapter 15
Do You Believe in Monsters?

"Dad, what have the living dead kids been doing since I've been gone?"

"Destroying our street. Take a look."

I peeled back the blinds. It looked like daylight outside. My street was lit up like a Christmas tree. "How is it daytime when it is nighttime?"

"Patches used the pumpkin cane to cast a spell that turned night into day."

"Oh." The next thing I saw was a guy lying face down on our front porch. He had a bloody knife sticking out of his back.

"Who is dead on the porch?"

"That's Mr. Wolasul. God rest his soul. Patches and his brothers chased him around the neighborhood. I tried to help. I even had the door open for him to come inside. But I had to close it when Sebastian threw a knife into his back."

"That's so messed up!"

"Yeah, it is."

I noticed another person lying at the end of our driveway. "My God! Who else is dead?"

"Old lady McMullen. She didn't make it either."

I shook my head in sadness. "Did Alina get away?"

"I think so. I haven't seen her."

"What happened to the fire-breathing horses?"

"I'm not sure. All I can say is ... they were there one minute then they weren't."

"Dad, that's so weird."

Just then Patches ran by. He was chasing Jimmy and Jay down the street. "Gonna get you, gonna get you!" he taunted them, laughing.

Aloysius joined in the evil fun, reaching out with his disfigured hands to grab the boys as he ran after them. "I bet you are dying to eat some of my Halloween candy!" he shouted.

Jimmy turned his head. "We don't want any candy! Leave us alone!"

"Ha ha ha," Aloysius laughed. "I hand-picked the candy from hell ... just for you." He threw it at Jimmy and Jay's feet. Every time a piece hit the ground it exploded like a firecracker. The boys jumped high into the air again and again until they wiped out.

Aloysius and Patches caught up and stood over my friends. Patches swung the pumpkin cane down, beating the boys with it. Every blow looked like sheer misery. My brothers screamed in pain.

"Dad, we gotta do something! He's beating them to death!"

"Johnny, take the shot."

I couldn't stand it anymore. The living dead kids had to be stopped. I yelled out the window as loud as I could, "Leave my brothers alone!" Then I fired twice. Patches lost his balance. He dropped the pumpkin cane and fell backwards into the grass. Aloysius helped his partner in crime back onto his feet.

"Who shot me?" Patches shouted, holding onto his right shoulder. "I thought we were immortal!"

"The boy in the window," Aloysius answered.

Patches stared at me. I felt happy. I had gotten him to stop hitting my brothers. "I shot Patches," I proudly exclaimed.

"Great shot, son. I don't know why I keep missing. Do it again. Kill them!"

Patches and Aloysius were now heading our way, and they looked very pissed off. I hated how their eyes burned with fire and their alive dead bodies made me cringe. Jay and Jimmy were still moving-beat up, but at least not dead.

Ding dong. Ding dong. The doorbell rang. "Who is at the door? And how is the doorbell ringing? The power is out," Dad stated.

"Roden! Open the door! Your time has come ... to die!" Sebastian howled.

"*Grrr!* Stop it!" Dad responded. He blasted at the door, causing two shotgun holes to appear.

I stopped him from firing again. "Don't waste the bullets. Shoot only when we can see, them."

He pointed his shotgun out the window, I followed his lead with the rifle. A frenzy of bullets flew toward the two Bibimtaff brothers. Aloysius took a hit to the leg, causing him to have to drag it behind him.

"Enough of this bullshit!" Patches screamed, raising the pumpkin cane high in the air. "Awake! Arise! Awake! Arise!" The eyes of the jack-o'-lantern turned fluorescent green. "Summon the monsters of Halloween!" The cane began to spin in his hand. Faster and faster it whirled until he couldn't hold it any longer. Then it flew away into a now transformed blood-red sky.

"This doesn't look good, Dad."

"Let's wait and see what happens, son."

We watched the pumpkin cane fly to the house at the corner of our street. It descended from above to tap the jack-o'-lantern on the porch. Then the cane moved on to the next house to make contact with its jack-o'-lantern. Every single jack-o'-lantern on the street was tapped by the cane. Finally, it came toward us. We did our best to destroy the cane with bullets but missed every time. Our jack-o-'lantern was touched, too.

When it was done, the cane flew back into Patch's hand. A big full moon appeared in the sky. I swear I saw a shadow of the giant devil man in the moon, and he was smiling. "Live! Live! Live!" Patch's commanded with his arms stretched high.

The jack-o'-lanterns on all our neighbors' porches began to grow long bodies with green vine torsos, leafy arms, legs, feet, and hands. The jack-o'-lantern monsters stood up. Their scary candlelit faces had been carved from every kid's Halloween nightmares.

I shot Dad a ghastly expression. *"Uh oh!"* I uttered.

"This is very bad," my father conceded, wearing the same ghastly expression on his face.

The jack-o'-lantern monsters ripped the front doors off every house and hurled the doors into the street. The monsters entered. We heard windows and furniture breaking inside. People screamed. Most ran out of their houses like chickens with their heads cut off. Someone or something pounded on our front door. The pounding got louder and louder until I heard a crack, and a weed fist-punched its way through the middle of the door. The door was then pulled back and ripped right off our house. Dad whispered, "We gotta hide and quick."

"We don't have time to pick a good spot," I replied. That thing is coming in any second now."

"Follow me," Dad said.

We entered the coat closet.

The monster ducked through the doorway, its jack-o'-lantern head almost hitting the ceiling. The creature kicked the hutch with its huge leafy foot. The hutch flew through the air and smashed into pieces against the wall.

Dad found a flashlight and shined it next to his chin. He looked as if he was about to tell a ghost story. I felt cramped standing against all the coats in the closet.

"You, okay, Johnny," Dad whispered.

"Yeah. We gotta slay that monster," I replied.

Chapter 16
Johnny's World

Dad shined the flashlight through the crack in the coat closet door. We were able to see only a little bit. The jack-o'-lantern monster was searching the living room up and down. I think it was trying to find us. When it couldn't, it shrieked which sounded like a blaring siren. Dad and I covered our ears. The noise was so loud that I thought my eardrums would pop.

The monster went into a rage. It smashed everything in the room. Leafy hands picked up the TV and threw it against the wall. Our grand piano played a few notes as it was broken apart. The bookshelf was torn down, spilling hundreds of books onto the floor. The glass coffee table shattered as a leafy foot went through it. Our couch and my favorite purple chair toppled over.

I heard a blood-curdling scream. "Oh my God! Your mom, she woke up," Dad said. The jack-o'-lantern monster must have had her cornered.

"Dad, we gotta go out there!" I whispered.

"Is your gun loaded?" Dad asked.

"I'm ready."

"One of us has to distract the monster so the other can shoot it."

"Great idea, Dad. Since I can run faster than you, I volunteer."

Dad put out his fist. I bumped it with mine.

"On three we go."

"Ok," I agreed.

"One, two, three." We opened the door. The jack-o'-lantern monster was about to grab my mom. She was cowering as its plant hands reached out. Dad ran behind the monster, and I ran in front of it.

"Leave my mom alone!" I yelled.

It turned toward me, tilting its head to the left then right. "Shoot it, Dad!" I war-cried.

A blast rang out. The jack-o'-lantern monster's head exploded, and its plant body collapsed onto the floor. Dad gave Mom a long hug, and she cried in his arms. I hugged her, too. "Lynn, honey, go back upstairs. Johnny and I need to fight the monsters. They are everywhere."

"Thank you, boys, for saving me."

"You're welcome, Mom. We love you."

"Lynn, don't come out anymore. I will come get you when it's time." Mom gave Dad and me kisses then headed upstairs. Dad grinned at me. "I finally hit one, son."

"You did great. Look at the orange pumpkin guts spattered on the walls!"

"Johnny, let's see what's going on outside." We looked out the window. Our street was a war zone. The jack-o'-lantern monsters had killed some more people. Dead neighbors lay in the street. It was too hard to tell which ones. We didn't see any other people. Whoever was still alive was nowhere to be found. They must have escaped or gone into hiding. The monsters roamed the road in search of new victims. "Where are the living dead kids?" he wondered.

"Yeah, Dad. Where did they go?"

"I need a closer look." He stuck his head out the window.

"I wouldn't do–"

"He he. We are right here, Roden," Aloysius snickered. He latched onto Dad and yanked him out of the window. Dad squirmed, trying to break free. He clutched the shotgun. Sebastian punched him in the face then he and Patches forced my father to his feet. Dad kicked Sebastian in the stomach, causing him to tumble to the ground. Patches waved the pumpkin cane through the air. Tiny bolts of lightning zapped from the jack-o'-lantern atop the cane.

"I don't think so." Dad ripped the cane from Patches' hand and tossed it as far away as he could. He put the shotgun up to the Bibimtaff brother's head. They wrestled for it.

"Don't resist! We are taking you back to Hell with us," Patches declared with a psycho smile on his face.

My heart was beating a million times a minute as I watched from the window. Dad and Patches kept struggling for the gun. Finally, Dad was able to free his right hand. He aimed and pulled the trigger. Bam! He shot Patches under the chin. "I don't understand! A shotgun blast this close should have blown you in half. Why didn't it?" Dad asked angrily as he stared into the evil brother's fiery eyes.

"Because I am immortal. This is not your world. Now get off me!" Patches threw Dad away from his body. Dad lay there in a defeated daze that only lasted for a moment. Aloysius and

Sebastian jumped on him, pinning him to the ground. Meanwhile, Patches got up and retrieved the pumpkin cane.

I couldn't let them take my Dad to Hell. What would I tell Mom? Running outside, I waved the rifle I was holding at Sebastian and Aloysius.

"Run, Johnny! Run!" shouted Dad.

Aloysius stepped on Dad's hands. "Shut up, Roden!"

"Let my dad go!"

"Look who's here. It's Johnny, Sebastian."

"Hello, Johnny," Aloysius sneered.

"You've got three seconds to get off my dad."

"No!" Sebastian snapped before slapping Roden in the face. What are you going to do now, Johnny?"

"I'm going to shoot you."

"You can't kill us. We are already dead."

I smiled coldly, took aim, and shot Sebastian in the face. His eyes burned out, and he fell over.

"Johnny, what the fuck? You killed my brother. He will be coming for him soon. How did you do that? Your Dad shot Patches at point-blank and nothing happened," Aloysius whined.

"Because this is *my* world!" I bellowed.

Chapter 17
The Devil's Moon

The ground began to split apart. A giant skeleton hand reached out and grabbed Sebastian. It pulled him under the earth then disappeared with the Bibimtaff brother.

"Get off my dad," I commanded.

"Okay. Okay." Aloysius raised his hands and released Roden.

"Johnny, behind you!" Dad yelled, pulling himself to his feet.

I whirled around to face a jack-o'-lantern monster. It screamed like a siren before ripping the rifle out of my hands and eating it. Chomp. Chomp. Metal broke in its fiery teeth. "Oh shit!" I exclaimed. I started to run but something slithering on my right leg stopped me. It was a pumpkin vine.

"I'm coming, Johnny!" Dad shouted while running toward me.

Patches waved the pumpkin cane through the air.

"Don't waste the magic. I got this," Aloysius told his brother.

He tackled Roden to the ground. "This is for Sebastian!" he yelled insanely, punching Dad countless times in the face.

There was nothing I could do. The jack-o'-lantern monster was about to eat me. Patches looked so happy as he watched both Dad and me in pain. I looked up into the reddened sky. The giant devil man was laughing in the moon.

Moments later he flew with flapping wings toward us. *"Ahhh!"* I screamed, as the monster lifted me toward his crushing jaws of fire.

Suddenly, a loud boom rang out. The monster had fallen over, and I fell on top of it.

Out of nowhere Sister Mary appeared. She reached her hand out to help me up. She held a long, smoking gun. I gave her a big smile. "Sister Mary, my dad needs help."

From out of the shadows walked Jimmy and Jay. They pushed Colonel Custer's wheelchair. The colonel, dressed in a military uniform, clutched a bag of grenades. My brothers were still wearing their Halloween costumes, but they were also armed with machine guns. The Terrible O and Poison Maker were here to save the day. I whistled. "Yes, the Cavalry is here!"

More jack-o'-lantern monsters surrounded us. The giant devil man was circling the sky right above. I wondered how he flew so fast from the moon.

"Let Johnny's dad go!" demanded Jimmy, as he and Jay pointed their guns at Patches and Aloysius.

At the same time Sister Mary started blasting jack-o'-lantern monsters. The colonel threw grenades. Monsters exploded everywhere. The giant devil man touched down and the ground shook. *"Raaaaa!"* he raged. He slapped Sister Mary to the ground and pushed over the colonel's wheelchair.

"I told you he would be coming," said Aloysius.

Jay and Jimmy opened fire on the devil man. The bullets bounced off his reddened, armor-like skin. He stuck out his three tongues. Two slithered at least twenty feet, reaching my brothers. The tongues picked up the boys and slammed them into each other. My brothers dropped their machine guns and fell to the ground. They did not move. The tongues retracted, back into the devil man's mouth.

I tried to reason with the beast. "Why are you here?"

"Raaaaa!" he raged again. He shouted in a demonic voice. "Because that was the deal!" he shouted in a demonic voice. Laser-looking lights shot out of his fiery eyes and beamed onto the street. Heavy hooves pounded under the road. Asphalt broke apart as the lasers sliced the pavement, turning it into rubble. The fire-breathing horses leapt out of the freshly cut hole.

Aloysius and Patches threw Dad into the back of their wagon. Pumpkin vines spontaneously grew longer in order to wrap around Dad's body. Lying there, he looked over at vine-wrapped Kennedy and Sister Virginia. Patches hooked the black horses up to the wagon. Fire shot from their nostrils.

I fell to my knees. "Giant devil man, please, don't take my dad. Take me instead." I started to cry. Pools of tears soon rushed down my face.

"I don't want you. *Raaa!*" he screamed, his claw fists shaking and pitchfork tail whipping through the air.

"Why are you doing this?" I pleaded again.

"Lucille! Lucille! Lucille!" he continued to rage.

Patches and Aloysius got into the wagon. It raced along the street toward the hole, which looked bottomless. The crazy vehicle flew straight down until I couldn't see it anymore. *"Nooooo!"* I screamed.

A thunderous explosion erupted from the bottomless pit. The sound knocked me over. The hole closed. The wagon was gone for good and so was my dad. The giant devil man laughed loudly and evilly. *"Ha ha ha! Ha ha ha!"* He flew away into the sky. Faces of jack-o'-lantern monsters appeared all around me. I felt their leafy limbs tearing at my body. Then a bright light carried me away.

"Johnny, wake up," Mom urged, opening the blinds. I poked my head out from underneath the covers and opened my sand-encrusted eyes.

"Happy Halloween," she said.

I yawned. "Is it really Halloween?"

"Yes, Johnny. It is Halloween."

I rubbed my head. "I just had the strangest dream I ever had. Is Dad okay?"

"Yes, he's fine. He got back from his trip late last night. He's sleeping."

"Are we going pumpkin-picking?"

Mom sadly shook her head. "There are no pumpkins for Halloween this year. No one knows why."

About The Author

Walter Friend lives with his wife and daughter in the peaceful town of Southington, CT.

"I have been writing stories and poetry for thirty five years. Story telling is my passion.

More original stories coming soon ..."

Made in the USA
Middletown, DE
10 December 2018